His Voice

HIS VOICE

A Memoir

by

Rima Pande

Publishing Facilitation: AuthorsUpFront

The Write Place
A Publishing Initiative by Crossword Bookstores Ltd.
Umang Tower, 2nd Floor, Mindspace, Off Link Road,
Malad West, Mumbai 400064, India.

Web: www.TheWritePlace.in
Facebook: TheWritePlace.in
Twitter: @WritePlacePub
Instagram: @WritePlacePub

*A salute to my mother
and all the strong and silent caregivers in this world
there are many*

*To all who were part of my father's circle of love,
I am forever grateful*

Contents

Foreword

संत हृदय

(Heart of a Saint)

चिर निद्रा में लीन हो गए भुला के सब संबंध
चेहरे पे है वही शांत, प्रसन्न, सौम्य भाव
कह रहे हो मानो मुझ से
जो कुछ पढ़ते सुनते आयी हो, उसी पे मनन करते
करना जीवन यापन

You have gone to sleep forever, forgetting all your bonds
Your face still has the same peaceful happy expression
It's almost like you are saying to me
Live your life based on everything you have studied
and learnt over the years

उत्तरदायित्व, कर्त्तव्य, कर्म के थे तुम उपासक
जिसको किया तुमने अक्षरशः सत्य
जहां भी गए पाया प्यार और सम्मान ही
मेरे जीवन का आधार थे तुम सदा ही

You were a disciple of responsibility, duty, work
And you always followed the truth

You found respect wherever you went
You were the foundation of my life

प्रभु ने सदा ही हमारा साथ निभाया
न जाने जीवन के अंत में क्यों उसने तुम्हे
लाचार व बेबस बनाया
फिर भी तुम हमेशा मुस्कुराते रहे
कभी हार न मान प्रयत्नशील होते रहे

God always supported us
I don't know why He made you helpless and weak
at the end of your life
Even then you kept smiling always
You never gave up and kept trying

अब प्रभु ने तुम्हे अपनी शरण में बुलाया
दो वर्ष की यातना से मुक्त कराया
पर मन तो विह्हल है, पूरा जीवन संभालना है
मुझे अब पुरानी यादों के सहारे जीना है
बस इस दुविधा से मन कभी न पायेगा उभर
दो वर्ष क्यों जिये तुम विवशता और पीड़ा का जीवन

Now God has called you to His protection
Liberated you from two years of suffering
But my mind is in turmoil, I need to live the rest of my life
I will live with the support of old memories
I will never emerge out of this quandary
Of why you of all people had to live with pain
and helplessness for two years

I travel back in time when my little girl would make up short stories and narrate fictitious anecdotes from the rear seat of the car. My husband and I would laugh, enjoying her mental awakening, feeling proud to have been blessed with this bundle of joy. Rima continued to dabble in poetic verses, but focused on academic excellence and a career, as well as being a wife and doting mother, though not being a disciplinarian like me, as she has often let me know!

It was a surprise, no doubt a pleasant one, when Rima revealed that she had a manuscript ready. When she said that the book is somehow somewhere a foggy mirror of her father's life, I was touched. I wondered how she would write about a person who I as a wife understood slowly with time, as I learnt to understand the enigma he was, admire his spirituality, appreciate his subtle humour, adapt to his simplicity, and be 'a worry worry' to his calm. A man always ready with a sympathetic hand extended to one and all, and above all possessing that rare virtue of being a patient listener unruffled by the pressures and upheavals of life; at least that is how he stood for and by me.

Rima has been a wonderful daughter, especially close to her father, for whom perhaps she was the dearest person. I wonder whether her understanding of him finds reflection in her writing.

It gives me immense pride and satisfaction to be writing this foreword to my daughter's book. I wish her all success and bless her on behalf of her father as well.

Harshi Pande

Preface

My father had two successive strokes within a month, leaving him paralysed neck down and unable to speak. For two years, my mother served him selflessly, supported by amazing family, friends, and helpers. She set a positive, respectful, uplifting, happy tone in my father's home hospital room, and everyone followed her lead. He was surrounded by people, music, and conversation. During this period, I spent many weeks with them. We stared at the constantly changing expressions on his face for clues – was he too hot, too cold, in pain, hungry, uncomfortable, attentive, tired, sleepy, somewhat happy? Well, maybe. We looked deeply into his eyes, searching for direction, pretending to understand what he would like us to do, doing it, and then searching for an almost imperceptible head nod of approval – did we get it right? Maybe. When he slept, I often stared at his face, wondering what was going through his mind, imagining the tumultuous flow of thoughts and emotions, trying to immerse myself in his stream of consciousness.

This book is a fictionalized, first-person narrative of my father's unspoken thoughts and observations during the two tumultuous years he was bedridden, interspersed with memories of key life experiences going all the way back to his childhood. This is my effort at diving into his mind, pretending to be him, imagining how he is thinking about his current situation as well as reflecting on his life in general, and capturing the swirl of emotions coursing through his mind as he thoughtfully deals with a crisis where he has completely lost control of his life. The glimpses into his life story are based on the anecdotes that got told and retold in the family, conversations with him prior to his stroke, and later with family and friends. I have taken many liberties, filling in facts and dates, but more importantly, in taking on his persona. Every one of us has a unique story. This is my father's, and I am proud to tell it.

Rima Pande

Prologue

11 March 2012

There is a silver hue to the shadowy faces that float above me. Caring, concerned faces. Khushi, Amiya, Devender, Sampreet, Rajesh, two more. Someone talks to me, a warm hand grasps mine, another soothes my brow. A cool drop of water touches my lips, delivered not by the metallic touch of a spoon but by the fragrant tickle of a tulsi leaf. 'Ganga jal,' whispers Khushi in a shaky voice. I hear the jarring jingle of the phone far away and loud muffled voices. All of a sudden, I realize that Amiya is talking to me; I feel her face close to mine, though her voice seems far away.

My name is Agastya Raj. I am seventy-five years old. My life's gradual descent began twenty-one years ago after a seizure. Soon after, my mind started to play strange tricks on me, going blank for a few seconds – randomly, without notice. I would often turn still and stare strangely without responding to questions, in a frozen state of either suspension or repeated action during these episodes. I would break into a cold, silent sweat after every episode.

It was frightening and disturbing every time – a complete loss of oneself for a few minutes – with no thoughts, no control of actions, and no recollection thereafter. All these years, the unspoken question that constantly nagged me – *What if ...? What if, I had a memory lapse while driving? What if, I blacked out while crossing the street? While in a meeting? While signing a cheque?* I tried to predict these blank moments – that way I could stop pouring tea or pause while crossing a busy road, to let the moment pass. I tried not to think about it, worry about when it might happen again. But I was not able to shrug off this dark cloud at any point in time.

Life around me continued at its usual pace. While I crossed my fingers behind my back every day and at every encounter, there were the moments of extreme joy and pride that did lift me out of my personal fog and and I was carried along in the general happiness.

Memories have kept me going. Memories I wrote about every day in my little notebook. Memories I quickly tried to remember after every blank episode, relieved and thankful that the spark that fizzled through my head for thirty seconds did not wipe out anything precious. Memories that gave me a reason to smile as I struggled to balance a chequebook, or deal with the chaos in the flat as the maid rushed through making dust fly with her broom, and then settling it back down with a mop, a fruitless exercise that was repeated every day in an effort to combat the incessant heat and dust of Delhi.

Memories that seem hazy sometimes, as my mind slowed down under the subtle pressure of the Dilantin that coursed through my blood, never in the right place when the electricity zapped through for thirty seconds, but incessantly thickening my senses otherwise. Memories that pushed me through the frustrations of my unpredictable state and pulled me above the mediocrity of my unremarkable days. Strangely, I even have memories of my mind when it was buzzing with activity and desire and excitement, driving a young man towards his lofty goals.

Two years ago, the temporary short circuiting in my head took on a monstrous new mutation. My mind was zapped in one wanton episode, leaving my legs useless. Another event followed within a few weeks, detaching all connections between my mind and body. My mind no longer controls my body, everyone else around me does. And every thought I have had in the past two years has stayed in my head, unable to be uttered.

I have tried. Very hard. For nineteen years, I lived with the uncertainty of mini seizures that created havoc in my mind. And for the past two years, I have been helplessly paralysed. Now I am tired. I am ready to move on. There is no fear or panic or regret, just a sense of peace and finality and withdrawal. Every actor has an exit cue. The show goes on, but actors who have no role to play cannot sit on the stage forever. They get in the way of life. Right now, I am that actor. I have been holding centre stage, immobile in my hospital bed, for two long years.

'A gentle goodbye hug from Sowmya,' Amiya says. I smile. This was what I was waiting for. A final bearhug from my daughter. One last long breath, an effort to make my last action on earth as whole as possible. With my eyes closed, I feel the inhalation, filling up my lungs. I am so deeply, deeply tired. This cannot go on any longer. And so, it does not … I exhale.

1

'Be a Good Patient, Papa'

'Accept the present in its totality.'

– Agastya Raj

March 2010

4 a.m. I watch the almost white Usha fan whirr at medium speed over the bed, making a soft clicking noise at each rotation, the silver circle in the centre undulating as the fan creaks with effort. I hear Khushi's deep but soft breathing as she sleeps, flat on her back as usual. I swing my feet off the bed, my feet clumsily sliding into slippers. As I stand up, my legs wobble alarmingly and I sit back down with a soft thud. Khushi opens her eyes.

'Everything okay?' she asks groggily.

'My legs seem to have gone to sleep.'

I try to stand up again, and manage to get myself upright.

'Okay now?' she says.

'Sure, go back to sleep,' I say, with a confidence I don't feel as Khushi drifts back to sleep. I make sure I stay close to a wall as I head to the bathroom and back to bed.

7 a.m. I still feel the need to hold on to something as I move around the house, opening the courtyard door to let in fresh air, brushing my teeth, sitting down for our morning cup of tea. My legs feel weak and unstable. *Maybe 18 holes of golf yesterday was not such a good idea – I am seventy-three, age is catching up.*

8 a.m. I finish a hot steaming cup of chai and munch on a Marie biscuit. Khushi and I discuss and plan the day as we usually do – meals, errands, visits. Background noises are increasing in tempo – the grating, annoying sound of the pump as it tries to push water all the way up to the fourth floor cement storage tanks; school buses, trucks, cars, bikes, and scooters all heading out for the day; street vendors throwing their voices to be heard over the din. I stand up to head to the bathroom. My legs crumple under me.

I ask Khushi to call Nawaz, the driver, inside, and they both help me to my room. I fumble a bit as I change my clothes while she calls the neurologist for an appointment. I focus my full attention on my wayward legs as I will myself to walk to the car.

I have my first ever wheelchair ride when we get to the hospital, as I am rushed to the MRI unit, the lab for blood work, and then to the doctor's office for nerve function tests. *Am I imagining it, or are my arms feeling weak too? Is the weakness spreading up through my body?* I swallow, drowning the panic I feel rising in my throat.

The MRI of the spine and brain rule out a stroke. I receive a diagnosis of GBS – Guillan Barre Syndrome. I settle into the CCU, hooked up to a bunch of monitors. An IV is inserted for immunoglobulin therapy, considered an effective therapy for GBS. The weakness in my legs is expected to continue to spread upwards, and I will be monitored in the CCU for a couple of days. There is some risk of breathing issues if the weakness spreads to my chest and makes my lungs weak, but the prognosis is good. My legs will be fine, and I will be back on the golf course after a few months of physical therapy. I am the healthiest patient in the CCU, and definitely the only one asking if I could get a television in my cubicle to watch the IPL Cricket Championship.

Visiting is limited in the CCU since a lot of patients are in critical condition, but I have the first cubicle next to the entrance and I also get marginally special treatment as Harveen's uncle. Harveen, a director at the hospital, is like a son to me. I grimace as I try to finish dinner, on a tray that is sitting on a wheeled table that hovers over my legs. I remind myself that I am too spoilt, too used to the fresh rotis Khushi serves right off the tava, and so I hold my comments. I talk to Khushi as she comes by for a few minutes before heading home for the night.

'How was dinner?' she asks.

'Well,' I say, trying to be positive, 'the dal was bland and soupy, the roti was a bit cold, but it wasn't bad.'

Harveen walks over after dinner from his on-campus home. 'I can't get you a TV in the CCU to watch cricket,' he jokes, 'but I brought you a book to read.' Harveen's cellphone beeps. It's Sowmya, calling from Boston. He chats with her reassuringly, giving her detailed information about my diagnosis and treatment, and hands over the phone to me.

I feel a warm feeling course through when I hear her voice. She talks to me cheerfully, effectively covering up any trace of worry.

'So, you finally get one of the experiences you missed in life so far – staying in a hospital,' she says. 'You are one lucky guy to make it to seventy-three without ever spending a night in one of those places.'

I nod, thinking how true that is. I have been blessed with wonderful physical health.

'Be a good patient, Papa,' Sowmya says. 'Remember, you are the healthiest patient in that CCU, which is why you are getting restless.'

I wish Harveen good night, thanking him politely for the book. *Conquering Everest* is an awe-inspiring account of a paraplegic's mountaineering adventure. I try and read, but it is a struggle to sit straight in the hospital bed and read in the dim light. I fall into a restless sleep, on an unfamiliar bed surrounded by unfamiliar sounds.

5:30 a.m. I open my eyes to see a nurse peering down at me. I respond sleepily to her greeting. My head feels heavy as she cranks up the bed and gets me a washcloth and toothbrush. The world seems to have kicked into slow motion. It seems like forever as I brush my teeth. My right hand trembles, my left hand feels leaden by my side, my legs seem not even there for me now. Something feels terribly wrong, except my fuddled brain cannot quite piece it together. I feel like I need to tell someone something, but am not quite sure what it is. *Must be the medication,* my brain thinks slowly. *Don't complain. Be a good patient. Maybe I need more rest.* I make no mention of how I feel to the nurse as I drift off to sleep again.

* * *

I wake up to the same beeping sounds and flickering fluorescent light above my face. There is an annoying tickle in my nose and my throat hurts. I reach up with my right arm to brush away whatever is tickling my nostrils. *Why does my arm weigh so much and have so much trouble working its way to my nose?* My fingers tremble as I scratch away at a piece of tape on my nose, unsuccessfully. My arm is tired now. As it drifts down, it grasps a plastic tube. Instinctively, I pull. *Ouch, that hurt.* I need a nap again.

When I open my eyes, a sea of attentive faces stares at me

expectantly. There seems to be some tension in the air. *Is that Sowmya? What is she doing here? She was in Boston when I went to bed last night.*

Khushi steps up to me. 'How are you feeling?' she says, speaking slowly and loudly. I wince, and nod an okay.

Then the stupid questions start. 'Where is Sowmya? Can you see her? Can you point to Sowmya?' I am confused and a little annoyed. *Of course I can see my daughter. Did I miss something?* The niggling feeling that something is going on gets stronger as the questions continue.

'Lift your right arm.'

I try, but it still feels heavy and clumsy.

'Lift your left arm.'

Of course, I nod, irritated, and do so impatiently. Nothing happens. I mean absolutely nothing. While my mind tells me I'm lifting it, my eyes see it lying there completely unmoving, almost lifeless. A cold shudder passes through me. *Is this a strange dream?*

'Lift your left leg.'

Nothing.

'Lift your right leg.'

Nothing.

The excitement I saw on the faces around me falters, frowns

appear, eyes darken, voices get a little subdued, even as the smiles stay pasted on everyone's faces.

Meanwhile, I concentrate my full attention on my limbs, willing them to move. *Move!* The mental effort I'm making should have my legs thrashing around like crazy beings, but they continue to lie there unaffected, indifferent, like soldiers on mutiny. There is a brief moment of hope as the doctor taps my big toe and I see it twitch, but that is quickly lost as a fog of panic sweeps through me, rising like a volcano bursting through my insides, making me hot, bothered, nauseated. It is now obvious that I am not waking up from an ordinary nap.

I look at Khushi, who looks confused but totally composed, and is nodding encouragingly at me. Sowmya is holding my right hand tightly.

'Sowmya,' I say, surprised by the low, hoarse whisper I hear. *I said that loud and clear, didn't I?* I clench my fists, both of them mentally, just one physically. *I need to figure this out. Calm down.*

Meanwhile, I am hungry. *How long has it been since I ate dinner last night? Was it last night?* The nurse brings over a white liquid in a glass jar and starts to pour into the end of a tube that I did not realize was leading to my nostril till I see the liquid rushing up my nose. *Now this is really annoying.* I frown and gesture at the tube, my right hand shaking with the effort. As my agitation visibly increases, there is a whispered discussion at the nursing station which is about 10 feet away directly in front of my bed, and the pipe is removed. After a few minutes, the nurse approaches again, holding a bowl with what looks like khichdi. I open my mouth for the spoonful that approaches but get nothing in except some dry air. I feel the warmth of the khichdi as it drops on my thin hospital gown. My mouth seems a little disassociated from my mind as well, not just my limbs. I concentrate again, this time with some success. The bland khichdi feels like fire as it courses down my throat. I close my eyes and let it pass. An hour later we have managed to get through most of the khichdi.

I gesture my need to use the toilet, pointing vigorously at the CCU bathroom. Again, there is a flurry of activity and discussion. The nurse brings me a small urine pod. I shake my head and refuse it. Finally, two ward boys move me to a wheelchair with a gaping hole in the centre and wheel me into the bathroom and reverse my wheelchair directly onto the toilet. Then they stand there and chat casually. I wait for them to leave.

'Didi asked us to stay,' says one, in response to my questioning look.

For the first time in probably seventy years, I take care of my business without privacy. It gets worse as I realize how little I can do and how I actually do need them there. They chat casually, to me and each other – cricket, movies, are you doing okay, all in one conversation. It gives a strange semblance of ordinariness to what, to me, is a very demeaning moment.

* * *

Crawl, walk, run … transfer. A new mode of mobility has been added to my vocabulary. Transferring is the process by which two able young men move a person from a bed to a wheelchair and vice versa, while the helpless person being transferred says a silent prayer each time and hopes to make it.

As soon as I am back in the hospital bed after my adventure to the bathroom and first double transfer experience, I fall into an exhausted sleep.

The next few days are a blur. Meals take up a large part of my waking hours, as I struggle to eat and drink. Khushi or Sowmya seem to show up every couple of hours, armed with newspapers, magazines, old photo albums, always looking extra bright and cheerful. Various doctors visit. Therapists float in and out, tapping and moving my limbs. Everyone talks in quiet tones and nods a lot. People keep asking questions, some more subtle and casual, some more direct and blunt than others. *Can I read? Do I remember people and events? Do I understand what they are saying?* Once a day I transfer into a wheelchair and go (or should I say get taken) to the grassy area outside the CCU.

The questions keep coming, casual, but as usual, always

accompanied by an intense glance that I am not supposed to notice. 'How many pigeons are at the fountain? Who is that coming? Do you remember when …?'

Everyone is having conversations around me – family, friends, doctors – and asking questions. But no one has actually explained anything to me. *Is anyone going to tell me what happened?* Perhaps they think I'm too fuzzy to understand, but now I've had enough. One day, when we are all sitting outside in the lawn, I ask abruptly, 'What is my actual condition?' sounding surprisingly loud and clear.

Khushi and Sowmya pause and look at each other. 'Sorry, we should have talked about it with you, just did not want you to worry,' says Khushi.

They explain it to me. I had a bilateral stroke, a somewhat atypical stroke where blood vessels on both sides of the brain get constricted at the same time. Since both sides of the body are affected, the typical drooping on one side that people associate with strokes does not happen. I nod as they speak.

I don't feel any fear or panic. The optimistic conversations about my legs recovering soon give me confidence. I am sure they will thaw out of this strange frozen state. At this point I can see them, but they don't belong to me. They may feel like two cylinders attached to my body, blocks of lead. But it's a temporary setback.

Something went wrong, but it can be fixed. I am going to walk again, because everyone wants me to walk again, because everyone says I'm going to walk again. I am looking forward to starting full physical therapy at the rehab centre tomorrow. A few more days in the hospital and we will be sent home. Khushi is talking about how she'll need some help for a few weeks once we go home – she is already planning.

A day later, there is a flurry of activity, the CCU nurses wear big smiles as they greet me in the morning. 'You are being transferred to Heritage Ward,' says the head nurse. I have reached a milestone, leaving the CCU. And I am now being promoted to the relatively less serious hospital room.

Once I get to my room in Heritage Ward, I realize it is better. For one, there is a TV and I have a lot of cricket to catch up on. I quickly learn to work the remote with my almost normal right hand. And most importantly, I can now have my family around all the time. There is a narrow cot by the window next to the hospital bed where Khushi decides to sleep, and Sowmya quickly convinces the nurses that there is enough room for another cot near the other window against the other wall. Thus begins our family camp with three permanent residents and a number of visitors.

A lot of people call every day. Sowmya is forever answering

the phone. She says the same things over and over – he is better, he is eating, doing his exercises, not sure when he goes home. One day she throws the phone on the couch and says, 'Did you know how many people are concerned about you? I am beginning to feel like a telephone operator.' I smile, she starts laughing, and, for the first time since the stroke, I laugh. My throat is still sore, and a strange throaty sound emerges. It sounds strange, but feels good.

The new addition to the routine is two daily visits to the rehab centre, a place buzzing with activity, therapists in white coats, and lots of people in wheelchairs. The physical therapy is boring but not so bad. The young therapist reminds me of my nephew and is nice, except when he works my hamstrings. Not so sure about the occupational therapy. The first day they hand me a toy, some coloured wooden rings that I am supposed to put onto a circular pole stuck on a wooden base. I am extremely annoyed. I clench my fists and firmly shake my head, *I am not a child.* Khushi notices me muttering to myself and politely asks the therapist to try something else. They offer me another toy, one slightly more complicated, a four-year-old version of the two-year-old toy they had given me earlier. I refuse to touch it. I am really upset. We go back to the room, where I fret over the insult, and feel bad as I'm fed my lunch.

Overall, the three weeks in Heritage Ward are strangely happy. I am surrounded by love and concern. My family feeds me, makes sure I take my medicines, keeps me laughing and engaged with conversation, movies, and music, accompanies me to the rehab centre twice a day for an outing, and encourages me to keep my right arm moving, writing, drawing, exercising through the day.

One night, while we are asleep, I suddenly hear a loud yell. I open my eyes to see Sowmya jumping on her narrow folding cot and gesturing at the floor.

'Papa, chuha! Do something!'

This is what Sowmya always did when she saw a lizard or a spider in her room as a child, yelling for help instinctively.

'I really cannot, beta,' I reply, laughing. 'Just say "Om Ganeshaye Namah" and maybe Ganesh will call his ride back.'

Ganesh doesn't appear. Instead, the ward boy on duty hears the noise and shoos the mouse from the room. We dissolve into a strange mix of laughter tinged with sadness, as it dawns on me that, for the first time ever, I cannot drive away my daughter's monsters. And as she hugs me, she realizes the same.

2

The Child is Father to the Man

'Why fit in when you were born to stand out.'

– Dr Seuss

1936–1956

The distinct, musty fragrance of pathis dominated my childhood memories. They lined the low brick exterior walls of many homes as they dried, or smoked and crackled in the open-fire stoves. Their smell was always in the air. Running up and down the intricate web of galis between the tightly packed homes, I ducked between grown-ups – men with turbaned heads and flowing kurtas striding along confidently, women with heads covered and eyes lowered, glancing away to avoid eye contact with men, often slowing down and stepping sideways. Jostling respectfully through groups of adults, keeping up with my brothers who were three and five years older, skipping sideways over the clean but open drains on each side of the gali to both give way and to get ahead. I was fascinated with the edgy shadows that morphed and ebbed as people walked through, created by the sun shining through the jagged edges of the rooftops and railings during the day, and at night, by the dim and intermittent light of kerosene lanterns hung on hooks at doorways or through windows.

I would come to a screeching halt at the huge, ornately carved set of wooden doors that led to Pande Nivas. My brothers would push and the door would grudgingly yield, placing us in the red-tiled foyer that offered many options – to the left, a stairway to the second floor and a U-turn to the open air kitchen area, to the right, an entry door into the baithak and dining room, or a step into the berra straight ahead. The berra was the nucleus of the home and the family – a large open area that throbbed with people and energy. The larger, more important, and nicer rooms were in the front – the baithak where the men of the family congregated to discuss important matters and where visitors were greeted, the dining room where the main family members were served their meals. The smaller, less important rooms were in the back – rooms allotted to distant family members who had nowhere else to go, and rows of storage rooms lined with grains and pickles.

Circling the berra on the second floor was a veranda that wrapped around the inside of the second floor and was surrounded by the family bedrooms and living quarters. The centerpiece of the berra was the large tulsi plant – a standard fixture in most households – ensconced in a large custom brick pot.

The third floor was the chhat, a flat open area. In summer, the chhat was watered down every summer evening to cool the rooms below. Khaats were put out for those who wanted to forsake the hot rooms to sleep under the stars in relative comfort. In winter, the chhat was used for various activities that migrated up from the berra. There were sheets spread with washed wheat and spices before grinding, fresh vegetables being dried prior to pickling, and freshly rolled papad drying before being packed in airtight containers. There were now rows of large earthen martvans containing mangoes, lemons, radishes, carrots, and cauliflowers pickled in mustard oil, that would continue to cook and mature in the gentle winter sun. The khaats stayed in winter. Every afternoon, the women of the household sunned themselves, cleaning and chopping saag, shelling peas, sewing, knitting, and chatting. The evening saw a transition, as the women migrated down, to take care of dinner and children, and adult males congregated there, with angithis to buffer the sharp cool wind that emerged as the sun set.

Life was calm and uneventful. In my memories, it was idyllic. The rough edges of everyday life in the heat and dust getting blurred by the passage of time, into something softer. Walking to school with Baldev, Dharmender, and Vyom – many pairs of skinny legs in large khaki shorts, carrying or dragging a dusty canvas bag with a slate and pieces of chalk to practice handwriting and do sums. Playing outside the school room till a quick warning from whoever first spied Master Umruddin's old Hercules bicycle as he pedalled furiously from Nurmahal. Evenings spent hanging onto stories spun by Mata Ram, a blind man who spent the end of every day ensconced under the peepul tree outside the mandir, relating a never-ending set of tales, mainly from the Mahabharata, the Ramayana, and the Panchatantra, to the gaggle of kids who gathered, spellbound by the drama and flair, but as I later understood, subconsciously assimilating moral values that he skilfully imparted through his storytelling.

Another favourite activity that seems humdrum now, but was very exciting then was to hang out at the village railway station, watching people and goods arrive. In spring, we waited for the fresh sugarcane that arrived from our family farms, excited to be handed over the best stalks to chew on by the supervisor. In summer, we waited for the Chausa mangoes to be offloaded, often being rewarded with a mango each and a pat on our heads, scurrying off back home savouring the pulpy goodness, and then playing a tossing game with the gutli, entertainment that could last a couple of hours. In winter, we watched stacks of fresh sarson being loaded on. Nights were spent mostly on the chhat, stretched out on the khaat waiting for a blissful waft to lull you to sleep in summer, or cocooned deep into a rajai with a muffler wreathing one's head on the pillow to stay warm in winter. There were probably a handful of nights in January when it was so cold that all but a couple of us descended into the warmth of a second floor room.

Being the youngest among your siblings, cousins, and friends is glorious only in the misty eyes of grown-ups. In reality, it usually means going along with a lot of things without an opportunity to express an opinion – playing whatever games the other kids are playing, often getting knocked around the most, working the hardest and focusing the most to win the guli-danda championship, never being strong enough to beat the older kids at kabaddi.

In my case, it also meant being dressed up as Sita during the weeklong Ramlila performance at the annual Chhinj Mela. Held during the ten-day Navratri festival in October, the highlights of the mela were the wrestling championships in the specially created akhara where wrestlers from surrounding areas demonstrated their physical prowess. And the re-enactment of the Ramayan in nine acts every evening for nine days, culminating in a grand finale on Dussehra, the final day of the festival, when the destruction of a large facsimile of Ravan, the evil king, lit up the sky as the fireworks stuffed into the giant structure exploded in a dramatic crescendo, collapsing the statue. Girls were allowed to enjoy the mela, but acting on stage was frowned upon; thus boys performed all female roles. This was mortifying, and it seemed to me like the whole village was pointing at me and having a good laugh at my expense when I staggered onto the stage as Sita, tripping over my sari, trying desperately to look feminine while maintaining my young masculinity at the same time. But of course, no one asked me how I felt about it.

In hindsight, it cannot have been easy for Master Umruddin to teach a random assortment of boys ranging in age from five to ten in one homogenous group. The only infrastructure at his disposal was the single room with a blackboard painted on a wall and an outdoor classroom under a tree outside, where everyone moved when the room became unbearably hot. The only teaching tools available were his own knowledge of Urdu, basic arithmetic, varied levels of information on a variety of other subjects, and the force of his personality.

'Murga,' he would yell suddenly, zeroing in on a target, sometimes accurately identifying the boy who was responsible for the misdemeanour, but often getting it wrong. In either case, the designated 'naughty boy' was punished, and in the short term, everyone's attention would improve, and tricks would be put aside till Masterji was in a better mood. Watching Master Umruddin's methods of discipline made me silently grateful that I was a quiet, well-behaved student. I was also reluctantly aware that my family status prevented him from ever asking me to take a turn cleaning his dusty bicycle with my schoolbag, or wiping the blackboard, or any of the many small chores he assigned his students. Of course, there were other expectations that went with being part of 'the first family' in the village. There was an unwritten expectation that a handsome meal would be provided by my family at the annual school inspection. While my brothers seemed to be proud of our family status, I was always mortified at the attention, standing quietly with my eyes down when the school inspector patted me on the back, uncomfortable with being complimented for something I had not contributed to in any manner.

Even though our life was simple, it was an inescapable fact that our family had special status in the village, implicit in the respect with which other people in the village community interacted with us and explicit in how Chachaji was always consulted, even by the Panchayat village elders, and how his decisions or advice resonated throughout the village. And he took his role seriously, wielding his soft power with great thought and deliberation. Later, when I grew up and came across the saying 'With great power comes great responsibility', I was immediately reminded of Chachaji.

One day, there was a lot of activity in one of the rooms at the back of the house – I heard loud whispers and suppressed screams. A couple of women scurried in and out. I hovered in the berra. The men congregated casually in the baithak, but there was a tense undercurrent to the nonchalant conversation. As usual, Chachaji, my father's uncle and the undisputed head of the family, sat in the centre on the takht, leaning on a bolster pillow. His resonant voice inspired confidence that everything was well, but I had observed him enough to know, based on how often he stroked his thick moustache, that he was worried about something. My father Biraji sat meekly to the right, as usual speaking softly and minimally, and only when spoken to.

Suddenly, I felt a large, strong hand on my shoulder. 'Bhiga, take this clock and as soon as you hear a baby scream, make a note of the time.' I didn't ask questions – I mean, nobody did when Chachaji asked them to do something. His wish, stated or otherwise, was always a command; that was the motto the family lived by. This was the first real family responsibility I had been assigned. In fact, it might even have been the first time I realized that Chachaji did not just know of my existence, but also knew my name, and knew me well enough to entrust me with this level of authority. That is how, at the age of ten, I timed my niece's arrival into this world. This may not seem like a big deal, but considering how important it was to get the time of birth right for the janam patri, it seemed like her future was in my hands, in that rusty clock I watched intently for hours. Astrological charts were taken seriously in our family. Timing her moment of birth correctly could mean the difference between having all the stars aligned to bestow good luck and fortune on my little niece, while a small error might mean inaccuracy in her janam patri that would follow her through life.

So far, I had been not just the youngest, but also the darkest, skinniest, and quietest in the family, born when my parents were already in their early forties. I was not used to any attention, and happy to not draw any. I was used to being overlooked in the presence of my beautiful older sister, the one whose muffled screams were at this moment making me very restless, and two brothers, all of whom were fair-skinned, healthy, and good-looking in an acceptable Punjabi way.

My self-perceived personal stardom after the role I played in my niece's birth gave me the confidence to stop by the hatti one day on my way back from school. The hatti was the epicentre of the family business – not really a shop, but a room in the main bazaar where all meetings were held, decisions and transactions finalized, relating to money-lending and the innumerable fields and landholdings in far-flung areas of Punjab managed directly by the family. The walls were lined with large ledgers and rolls of paper used by Chachaji to keep track of the dues from the vast sugarcane farms and rented buildings in Jalandhar, as well as the money-lending transactions spawned by the cash-rich lending business. I wasn't sure how I would be received as I sidled in and stood awkwardly, as my father Biraji glanced nervously from me to Chachaji, waiting for a cue before saying anything.

I had heard that Chachaji and his friends, including the village doctor and the aspiring politician, played a game called chess every afternoon. And they were just starting. 'Do you want to watch, Bhiga?' asked Chachaji. While I nodded tentatively, Biraji relaxed visibly and refocused his attention on the large accounting khaata he was working on as I joined the audience for the chess game.

After that I stopped by regularly, no longer embarrassed by my forwardness but eager to sit proudly behind Chachaji as he systematically beat everyone. His opponents did not lose out of fear or respect, as their common love of chess made it an even playing field. Chachaji was just the best player. Everyone got used to my presence and slowly I became an accepted participant in the informal chess club, even playing with Chachaji when the group was not around.

At age twelve, my first day at the AS School in Jalandhar opened my eyes to the world beyond Shankar. During the one-hour train ride from the village, I stared out of the barred windows as we made our way past fields of sugarcane, wheat, bright mustard greens, rows of vegetables, and mango orchards. At school, I observed the city boys, their confidence and ambition, their lack of interest in the boys from the surrounding villages. More importantly, I was dazzled by the variety of teachers, subjects, and books, by the treasure of information and knowledge at my disposal.

With Bhabho's permission, I set myself up in the upstairs room of the small guest house across the narrow lane, which was connected to the main house by an overpass. Bhabho was the grand lady of the village, with a distinct style, her diminutive frame always upright, wrapped in crisply ironed saris. She was a strict parent, but had a soft spot for me, her youngest child. I started to spend hours in my new room, cocooned from the rest of the family, away from my brothers, disturbed only by the muffled sounds of people talking and the frequent squealing of the hand-pump in the courtyard when the guest room was occupied.

I would take the train home as soon as school finished, armed with books from the school library. I would creep upstairs to my room, unnoticed through the entrance on the other side of the hand-pump courtyard, and get lost in whichever historic, fictional, scientific, or mathematical world that caught my fancy. I wanted to read as much as possible before dinner, since I did not like squinting at my books in the dull light of the kerosene lamp, with my eyes watering and the smoke irritating my throat. The kerosene lamp was unavoidable during exams, but I managed to avoid it most other days.

Reading was easy; I enjoyed it and went to great lengths to find books. Besides the library, my friend Ved and I would often beg our families for a few annas for a special trip to a bookshop in Jalandhar. On one such trip, we got permission to spend the night at the Pandeyan di Sarai in Jalandhar, an inn that my family ran for travellers who could get dinner, a safe place to sleep, and a comfortable khaat for 2 annas a night.

Under my bed was also my greatest treasure – a set of

Meccano building blocks that had magically arrived from Kenya – a gift from my uncle. While my siblings chatted incessantly with cousins and friends who were always at our house, I would spend hours building bridges and seafaring ships, dreaming of the day when I would be commanding one of my own.

In 1947, independence from the British came to India as an experience more bitter than sweet. The fleeting joy at gaining independence after a long struggle was overshadowed by the mass migration, homelessness, and loss of life due to the arbitrary new borders that were sketched overnight between India and Pakistan. Our location in Eastern Punjab meant that we were buffered from the extreme chaos that hit Amritsar, Kapurthala, and Faridkot, the districts that suddenly had a new border with another country. As millions fled from one side of the border to the other, losing homes and families, I only remember intense huddled conversations around the new radiogram in the hatti, the only one in the village, the quiet disappearance of a few Muslim families to Pakistan, the sudden appearance of new Hindu and Sikh residents in their homes, the general pall of gloom that overshadowed any celebration of Independence, and the deliberately loud footsteps and whistles of the nightly patrols that continued for a few weeks after Partition to keep order in the village.

Our family fortunes were somewhat shaken by the Partition, but our precipitous financial downfall started with Chachaji's sudden death two years after. It created absolute chaos for the family business, as my father and his younger brothers struggled to make sense of the intricate web of landholdings and loans. Erstwhile friends and customers, taking advantage of the vacuum in knowledge and authority, suddenly became completely unaware and unhelpful. They promptly re-occupied lands they had mortgaged, forgot about loans they had taken, and claimed ownership of agricultural land they had been cultivating on a lease.

In the next two years, our family income completely dried up, and we watched helplessly as my father struggled in vain to establish control. Suddenly, the unstated assumption that we would all grow up to manage the family business vanished into thin air. My father and others around him had no understanding of life and options beyond the family business. My uncles went off to Africa to seek their fortune, literally. My older brother Sukhdev was sent off to the UK to study and train himself for a career beyond zamindari. The decision was not so much driven by a search for greater opportunity, but because it was the best option available. Even though our family fortunes had dwindled, the family reputation needed to be maintained. The logic was that Sukhdev would find a good job after getting a foreign degree, either in India or in the UK.

It was obvious how Chachaji's death had shaken or rather destroyed the family fortune, but the silent impact on me mostly went unnoticed. I spent the night after he died staring blankly at the stars, oblivious to the hushed voices downstairs, unable to sleep, with Dharmender on the khaat next to mine, in quiet support. The loss of my hero and mentor left me untethered for a while. I withdrew even more into my own room, concentrating even harder on my books and studies. My silent personal homage to him was my name on the Punjab University Merit List after the statewide board exam I took at the age of fifteen.

My father had never gone to college. Kids from rich business families in the early 1900s didn't go for higher education, they learnt the family business. Some education was good, too much might put other ideas into their heads. By the time I was finishing school, the family business had evaporated. And I really wanted to go to college, and figure out how to realize my unspoken dream to join the Navy.

Government College, Hoshiarpur was considered one of the best in Punjab, an institution that ironically benefited from the Partition, gathering in its folds the brain dump that came in the form of the teachers that fled Lahore.

I was very excited the day Biraji dropped me off at the college hostel, which was buzzing with activity. Heavy, metal trunks were somehow being moved up the narrow, musty stairs, while military-style canvas bedding rolls balanced on shoulders bumped into each other as people passed. After I had made two trips up getting my trunk and bedding to my room on the second floor, I waited impatiently as

Biraji slowly made his way up with two square covered pails full of pinnis that Bhabho had made for me as study fuel. In my excited seventeen-year-old state, I could not understand the slow shuffle of his sixty-two-year-old feet and his complete lack of enthusiasm at this big move of mine or the many opportunities around the corner. At the time I couldn't appreciate how the family bankruptcy weighed on him, how responsible he felt for not being able to keep the family business going, and how worried he was that I might not find a decent job even after he scraped money together for my college fees.

* * *

An image of Master Umruddin emerged in my head as I stepped into a classroom in front of a sea of young faces as a teacher. I was nineteen, and had just returned from college. This was a very different school from the one I started my education in – there were many classrooms and teachers, and the Punjabi language had been elevated to official status, replacing Urdu as the language of instruction after Partition. After my first day as a teacher, I meet my friend Vyom, who was also back home from college, preparing for his move to the U.S. to do biomedical research. He was completely taken aback when he heard that I had become a schoolteacher.

'It's temporary, I just needed something where I could earn some money while I apply to the Navy,' I explained to him.

We were at our usual spot, the peepul tree near the mandir, from where we could fleetingly watch a blurred version of the hit movie *Anarkali* being projected on a large white canvas screen set up in the makeshift open air theatre in the maidan.

The melodrama of the movie, the high-pitched voices and loud sound effects, faded into the background, as the image of myself as a Navy Commander, watching the sunset on the deck, dressed in a sharp white Navy uniform, flooded my mind. I had been dreaming of the Navy since I built ships with my Mecanno blocks, and now it seemed within my grasp.

3

'Don't Tell Anyone How Old I Am'

*'Do not allow wrong thoughts to enter your mind. Block them
as soon as they knock on your mental door.'*

– Agastya Raj

May 2010

Sowmya is leaving for Boston today, going straight from our Heritage camp to the airport.

'Good morning again, Papa,' she says, calling from the airport after checking in. 'Keep working hard. I will be back next month.'

I nod into the phone and can't help saying, 'I will miss you,' probably the first time in my life I have ever I articulated such a sentiment.

Life goes on in Heritage Ward. Every day, I bring up the issue of getting rid of the catheter hanging by my bed. Ironically, it seems to bother me more than the fact that both my legs and one arm cannot move. I just don't like it, especially when I have visitors. I can see their eyes hurriedly look the other way if their gaze falls on the plastic bag hanging by the side of the bed, collecting the yellow liquid trickling down constantly. Since it is the one question I whisper to the doctor during every morning and evening round when he asks if something is bothering me, it is finally getting attention and the catheter is removed. However, the mini celebration does not last long. It seems my bladder has forgotten to function. I feel like a two-year-old being encouraged to urinate on demand. And the humiliation increases when I cannot seem to comply. Then I have to undergo another embarrassing activity every few hours as I discover the verb form of catheterization. Not sure which is worse.

Meals are still slow and unsteady as I struggle to eat with my right hand alone. But I don't want help. I ignore Khushi reaching out to hold the spoon or glass as my hand shakes and spills, and continue to feed myself. I now realize the unacknowledged value of the left hand, the support role it quietly plays, while the right hand gets all the credit for getting things done.

Visits to the rehab centre are the highlight of the day. I have mixed feelings about rehab. It feels good to be getting out of the room and doing something twice a day that has a purpose. The only problem is that occupational therapy still makes me feel like a five-year-old – playing with blocks, the clapping, the words of encouragement. And the physical therapy just hurts. Every session ends with me asking to go back to my room, impatient and annoyed with my helplessness. 'This is your new job, and you need to do it with as much effort as your real one' – I keep reminding myself of Sowmya's friendly but serious instructions.

Visitors come by every day, and the phone calls continue. It felt good to hear from everyone when it first happened, but after a few days, it has become exhausting to hear Khushi repeat the same status, trying very hard to emphasize some minor improvement in what is actually a fairly constant state of affairs. I can also feel her annoyance and embarrassment and irritation at some of the thoughtless questions that people often ask.

Kids are different. 'Can you draw the sun, Bare Papa?' asks my niece's daughter, who has come to visit with her grandmother. Her tone is encouraging and concerned. Having noticed everyone's tendency to ask me questions and tell me to do things nowadays, she has taken on a role much coveted by a seven-year-old. Every time she visits, she becomes my 'teacher', instructing me to write and draw, as well as conducting a verbal quiz on general topics. I smile crookedly, gripping the pencil tightly as I draw a circle on the piece of clip-boarded paper she is holding in my lap. My hand pulsates with sharp pain, but I keep going, the smile on her face energizing my hand and spirit.

* * *

I wake up hot and trembling one night; despite the air-conditioning, the bed is wet with sweat. 'Khushi,' I whisper hoarsely, my head pounding. She sits up immediately on the low cot next to my bed and rings the bell. 'Fever,' says the nurse. The next day, the antibiotics take charge of the urinary tract infection I have developed. I feel better and rest the whole day, savouring a day off from the rehab centre.

My pounding head drowns out the beeping sounds around me as I struggle to open my eyes. *I must be dreaming*, I think, closing my eyes. *I seem to be back in CCU, in Bed 6.* I open my eyes again. I am really in Bed 6. I notice something. In addition to the annoying tube in my nose, there is also something covering my mouth. I raise my right hand to remove it, but cannot seem to move my arm at all. In fact, I am not even sure where my hand is. I open my mouth to speak, but nothing happens. *It must be that mask*, I assume, drifting back into a tired sleep.

The next time I wake up, my bed is raised a bit and I can look around. *I must be dreaming again.* I see two faces staring at me, vaguely familiar. My head begins to swim and I feel sick, so I close my eyes. Every time I open my eyes after that, there seems to be a different face looking down at me. I wish Face 1 and Face 2 would come back. I open my mouth to ask, but am at a loss for words.

Things are definitely wrong. I can sense it. I can see it in the worried looks, the tense, whispered conversations, the forced smiles. And I can feel it in my head, which feels like someone has poured cement into it, overwhelming my thoughts and constantly dragging down the few that manage to float to the surface. I struggle to figure out who is who, and what is what. I feel like I know, but all the information seems to have drowned in that cement that is still swirling and thickening in my head. I feel an emptiness in my stomach, but it takes some time to piece together the thought that I need food. After I put this thought together it still seems like a wasted effort, since the cement has also clogged my words and I have no idea how to tell someone that I am hungry.

I wake up to a soft hand touching mine. 'Nana?' says a young voice. My eyes fly open with excitement. *Good morning, sweety,* I smile as I see Rahul and Atul standing on either side of Bed 6. I reach out with my right arm to hold them, until it dawns on me that my right arm is now also disconnected and immobile, just like the other three limbs. I sense panic rising in me, so I close my eyes and descend into darkness.

Over the next few days I keep my eyes closed most of the time, as I try to sort through the jumble of faces and memories in my head. As I mentally grope for words. As I open my mouth and hope for a word. Everything seems disconnected. I am exhausted, frustrated, and scared. I constantly remind myself, *be a good patient.* I hear whispered conversations about a second stroke, but I am too tired to focus on the words, or figure out how to ask a question.

* * *

Khushi and Sowmya are standing on either side of my bed. Khushi is pressing a white envelope into my right hand, then picking up my hand and nudging it towards Sowmya. I know this because I see it happening – I don't actually feel the envelope or my hand being extended or Sowmya taking the envelope. Sowmya's face suddenly crumbles and she starts crying.

'I am sorry. I am so sorry I told you not to tell anyone how old I am. You can tell everyone. Please say something, Papa,' she sobs.

I stare at her blankly, not sure what she is talking about. *Who is old?*

'Did you wish her?' Khushi asks brightly. 'It's her birthday.'

I continue to stare at Sowmya as she rushes out, wiping her eyes.

I am fast asleep. Suddenly my head floats up and I open my eyes to see the bed being cranked and my body gathered by two young men – *How do I know that? How did that thought come into my head? That they are men, and they are young?* – and moved to a wheelchair. *Another word.* I am pleased with myself. A slight breeze wafts past me as the wheelchair makes its way through a long corridor, and out into the bright and hot sunlight. The chair wheels up a ramp outside a low brick-coloured house, and into a room with sofas on one side and a dining table on the other. *Lots of words.* I see a lot of smiling faces talking to each other. The trip seems to have cleared my mind a little. *Maybe the cement is being flushed away with the IV fluid pumped into me.* Suddenly, I put a lot of thoughts together with a speed that amazes me. *This is Harveen's house, I know all these people. That's a cake. Sowmya is cutting it with a knife. It is her birthday.* The relief I feel dissolves into a sudden feeling of sadness as I sit there mute, unable to say any of the above words, unable to share my happiness at putting it all together. My head bobs gently, floating on a body that apparently still belongs to me, but not to my arms or legs. I seek refuge the only way I can – I withdraw into a tired sleep.

4

London Calling

'Be grateful for the hard times, they just make you stronger.'

– Keanu Reeves

1957–1964

My first glimpse of London was dark and gloomy, as I stared out of the small round plastic window of the Air India flight. Or it may have been a reflection of my state of mind. Two months ago, my dream of joining the Indian Navy had been shaken by the fear and stress I saw in my father's eyes when I showed him the application form, dissolving completely in the tears that glistened on my mother's cheeks when I shared my plans with her. I retreated, thinking they would get used to the idea. But every time I mentioned the thought, they panicked. My parents had lived fairly insular lives, travelled only within 100 miles of their village, and had never seen the ocean. No one in our family had ever joined the armed forces. But for the fact that we were no longer rich landowners, a conversation about working for anyone or any kind of job would never have occurred. 'You are such a good student, a gold medallist, maybe you can become a college teacher,' said my father, his quiet voice sounding more uncertain and tentative than usual.

When your dreams collapse, you can feel the air beneath your wings disappear, and the wings that lifted you gently towards your dreams drop and solidify into a metal straightjacket that starts to strangle your breath. You want to run; get away, far away, fast enough to dislodge the weight. At that moment, I was unable to rise above the cacophony of disappointment swirling in my head to even consider what was actually a good idea, an academic career. I wanted to go far away, and at that moment, the farthest place on my horizon was the UK. Both my brothers had already been dispatched there. With the family in very bad shape financially, but still maintaining the mantle of respectability and sense of elitism that made it impossible to do a 'lowly' job in India, going to the UK was the most practical option. We could take up any kind of job, make significantly more money, live comfortably, and still send the parents some money to survive.

I was now being transported to an unknown and bleak future in an alien land, trying desperately to shut out the images of myself in a Navy uniform that kept popping in my head. The book of jokes I bought on my bike ride to Kashmere Gate with my close friend Dharmender did nothing to lift my spirits. The philosophic guidance of the Sukh Sagar and the Bhagavad Gita that my mother had given me before I left did nothing to calm my state of mind.

My mind remained clouded and confused. Should I have tried harder to convince my parents about my desire to join the Navy? Was there some way I could have convinced them that not every young man who joins the Armed Forces dies? How would they have responded and adjusted if I had insisted on following through with my plans? Where is the balance between following your dreams and filial obedience? I was filled with regret, but there was no going back. Biraji had taken a loan to buy my one-way ticket to the land of dreams, and even if I felt like I was living a nightmare, I would have to make the best of it.

Sukhdev, my older brother, was at the airport to greet me. He gave me a quick half-hug. 'All good? Biraji and Bhabho ok? You ate dinner on the plane, right?' he asked hopefully. He turned away to look for my suitcase even before I could respond. I had not eaten, my head was throbbing and my heart seemed to have dropped eight inches. Any frantic signals of hunger from my stomach were not making it through the dense despair that enveloped my mind and heart.

'The train to Wolverhampton is at 5 a.m.,' Sukhdev said casually. I glanced at my new HMT watch which I had set to London time – it was 10 p.m. 'I can show you a little bit of London,' he said, walking along as I followed.

My brother assumed that wandering around London all night after my 18-hour flight was perfectly fine. And as the youngest in the family, where the hierarchy of respect followed chronological age, the thought of protesting did not cross my mind. Also, I did not care. I remember very little of that night – just tired feet, aching arms, a loud smoky pub, fountains, wrought iron gates, and then the blessed comfort of a cushioned seat and the soothing chug-chug of the train.

In keeping with my mood, I was soon in Black Country. The area around Wolverhampton was permanently shrouded in a grey fog of pollution due to the heavy concentration of steel-making industries. I had moved from the vibrant colour film of my village to a black-and-white one, or rather a black-and-grey one, since white was hard to come by.

Again, I did not get much time to think about it. The next morning I got directions from Sukhdev to take a bus to the factory where he had already talked to one of his friends about me starting a job. The interview was perfunctory. It was not the kind of job that required the hiring person to know me or my skills. Mostly a quick glance to make sure my limbs were functional, my senses in order, and I could understand enough English to follow orders. I would be one of many pairs of hands that did what they were assigned over and over again on an assembly line for nine hours every day.

The first morning at the factory was the longest of my life.

When the lunch bell rang, I shuffled to the lunch room, my mind numb, my stomach growling with hunger. I picked up the tray, nodded thank you to the lady behind the counter when she put my lunch on it. The plate had a deep centre, and in the middle was something that looked like a big round samosa, open, with vegetables and brown chunks floating in it. In a bowl on the side were some potatoes that looked like they had been cooked too much and collapsed. In a mini-jug was a light brown liquid. Everyone around me sat down and started eating. The smell of the food made my stomach turn nauseous. I drank some water, then forced myself to eat a few spoons of the tasteless potatoes. I had to get through the next four hours.

My co-workers told me what it was – 'It's always Yorkshire pudding, gravy, meat, and potatoes. Trying hard to look different and interesting but tasting the same.' They laughed.

For the next few days, I ate two large parathas before leaving home, and avoided the lunch room. Slowly, over a couple of weeks, I got used to the lunchroom smell, gradually started to taste everything, and was soon wolfing down lunch, if not with relish, at least with full acceptance. Except for beef. Even though I was not a believer, my mind was unable to cross that deeply embedded barrier.

Initially, the order and predictability of the assembly line seemed to work as a defence mechanism against the thoughts and emotions raging in my head, at least while I was at the factory. Each mind-numbing day on the assembly line weighed me down, quelling thought and emotion. But soon the deadweight feeling that replaced the turmoil was even worse. In the evening, I usually went to bed before Sukhdev came back from the pub. I tossed and turned every night, still unable to clamp down my despair at the turn my life had taken. I was miserable, and the fact that one could take a bath only once a week when the landlady turned on the hot water added to my sense of misery. Through the first few months in the UK, the only thing that gave me some satisfaction was that I was able to send home £1–8 every week from my wages of £7–10.

I needed to change my robotic existence before it slowly killed my spirit. I might never command a ship in the Navy, but I was definitely not going to spend my life on the assembly line. One day, I was visiting my childhood friend Vyom, who had recently moved to Birmingham to live with his brother Braj. Vyom was excited, describing his plans to study for a PhD when I realized what I needed to do. If I was to pull myself off the factory floor I had to study. And if I was going to study, I needed to pick something I enjoyed.

In August 1958, I escaped my dark shadowy existence in Wolverhampton and moved to Birmingham, where I got reacquainted with sunlight and myself. Braj welcomed me into what would become my home for the next four years – not just a room to sleep in, but also a place where there was always a home-cooked meal waiting for me on the small kitchen table every day. I enrolled in London University in the BE (Bachelor of Engineering) programme and started studying. I chose engineering because it seemed to have good job prospects. Or maybe the Meccano blocks of my childhood had something to do with it. Life was just as busy, but so much better. The deadweight seemed to shift off my shoulders. The Shankar–Jalandhar train ride was replaced by the Birmingham–London commute, and I beamed at the bus conductor as I paid my fare three days a week.

'What's your name, lad?' he asked one day. 'Agastya,' I said, noting the frown as he tried to repeat it. 'Why don't you call me Raj?' I quickly continued, sharing my much easier middle name. His face immediately relaxed as he shook my hands and repeated what until now had been my middle name. Since that day, I became Raj – simpler, more manageable, more modern. It was amazing how much smoother each social encounter became when the person you were interacting with didn't have to go through the awkward ritual of trying very hard to get your name at least 80 per cent right.

My first friend in college, Ben, was a tall, thin and pleasant young Englishman. His enthusiasm, as well as my quiet but feverish desire to learn new things, resulted in all kinds of lessons. He became my unofficial mentor and coach, taught me swimming, tennis, and billiards. My social life improved further when I met Alok, a Bengali gentleman also taking classes at London University. We connected instantly. Alok often visited me in Birmingham, partly for Braj's good home-made food. We made outings to movies and dancehalls. There were always a number of pretty young women there, wearing nice dresses and looking like there was some purpose to their presence. It took us some time to figure out that girls who said they couldn't dance were just politely declining our overtures. However, our youthful enthusiasm meant that we were able to shrug off the refusals and keep asking until someone said yes. After all, we couldn't dance alone, and it seemed important to try out the foxtrot I had learnt from Ben. My third friend was Robin, who was a few years older, was somewhat more settled with a job and family, had a car, and often kindly included Alok and me in picnics and other such expeditions.

London University had given me a generous scholarship, Braj took care of food and lodging, and my brothers had let me off the hook for sending money home while I studied, but I still needed to make some money to cover my expenses.

'Since you are so English now, why don't you try potato picking!' said Ben. I thought he was joking until I discovered that picking potatoes was a much sought after summer job. Good pickers could earn a few pounds a day, depending on how quickly they could follow the tractor that threw up potatoes with its revolving fork attachment, collect them in steel buckets, and tip them into large sacks. The normal payment was a piecework rate of a half-a-crown per sack! Pickers were also permitted to take home a 'feed' or small bag of potatoes each day. In addition, the women from the farm brought out tea every morning and afternoon, as well as thick homemade sandwiches for lunch.

Picking potatoes eight hours a day will convince almost anyone of the value of a good education. The aches and pains of the first few days got me completely focused on getting my engineering degree as fast as possible. After six weeks, my back hurt permanently and my hands were coarse and dry, but I had saved enough money to get through many months of college and earned the respect of the farmer, even securing an invitation to come back next summer.

'Rhaaj.'

My heart dropped to my knees when she carefully repeated the name I had just offered to her as an introduction, frowning slightly as she tried to make sure she got it right. I had been watching her for many evenings but had just gathered up the courage to approach her in the dancehall.

'I would love to dance,' she said with a smile. I willed my shaky knees to move, at the same time trying to remember the few moves I had picked up and practised with Ben.

Within a few minutes the strangeness evaporated. I found myself talking to her about myself, and to my joyous surprise, she listened intently. For the first time, someone was actually impressed that I was studying to be an engineer. As I talked to her, I felt there was a meaning to my studies beyond getting off the factory floor and into a glass-walled office. Instead of a mere dance partner, I felt like I had found a friend.

Amanda and I met for tea, took long walks, went to movies and talked, a lot. It was refreshing to find someone who had no pre-conceived social or cultural notions with which to interpret my thoughts and comments, but was interested in understanding me as a person. A friend who I could very rapidly see becoming an important part of my life. Until we talked about that, and realized that our simple relationship would most likely falter under cross-cultural burden and complexity if it evolved into anything beyond friendship. We accepted it for what it was, a temporary but wonderful time when our paths crossed in life, comfortable in the thought that that we would move on in the different directions that our lives were expected to take. Yet her photos remain in my album till today, even though Khushi has teased me for years about Amanda.

I had always wanted to go back home. Once Amanda got married and moved, and I was getting close to finishing my degree, I approached the goal with more focus. I started poring through the employment advertisements posted at the Exchange, often stopping there on my way to and from the station. One day, I saw an advertisement from an English company that made auto-electric parts and was recruiting engineers for its overseas operations, one of which was a factory being set up in Madras. I headed to the typing store to get my curriculum vitae and cover letter done, and mailed it out the same day. I started to imagine the joy on my parents' faces when I told them I might move back to India in a few months, the glimmer of hope that they would see one of their three sons back home.

Within a month, I had started what was to become a lifelong career. The freedom of having a real salary and being on my own was exhilarating. Someone in the personnel department found me digs near their Birmingham factory. The landlady was nice. She even turned on the hot water every evening for an extra shilling a week in rent.

Within a couple of weeks of joining, I bumped into Alok, who coincidentally had joined the same company, also with the objective of moving back home. Over the next few months, I was introduced to a number of other young Indian men who had joined the 'overseas operations group' – Jeet, Amar, and Manoj – as we began a common journey that led us from a few months of training in Birmingham to the brand new factory complex in the suburbs of Madras, India.

5

Homecoming

'Ordinariness is a way of daily living. Harmonize with it in totality.'

– Agastya Raj

June 2010

I move from the CCU to Everest Ward the second time around, since Heritage Ward is full. Everest Ward is in an older building, the paint is grey, the floors scratched, the windows smaller, the rooms generally less cheerful. *A second-class ward for less successful patients*, I think bitterly. It does mean that I have my own room with a TV again. However, I realize soon enough that actually means less than I thought, since I am now unable to move, speak, use a remote, or tell anyone what I want to watch. *At least Khushi can stay in the room with me again, instead of sitting on the metal benches lining the corridor wall outside the CCU.*

Once I am 'settled' into Everest Ward after my second stint in the CCU, Sowmya once again departs from the hospital to fly back to Boston. Khushi completely takes over the task of taking care of me. We settle into a similar schedule to the one in Heritage Ward before my second stroke, with some major differences – I can do absolutely nothing, and all conversations are now one-sided. I am no longer doing as much as being done to.

* * *

It has been a bumpy ride propped up in the back seat of the Santro. It is hot and humid. The bright sun reflects off the sweaty sheen on faces as people scurry around outside. The roads look vaguely familiar. It feels like a long journey as the car stops, starts, weaves through traffic. I try to remember when I was last in a car, when I went to the hospital, but have no idea.

'We are going home today,' says Khushi, as she gently nudges me upright against her shoulder after the car takes a sharp turn. *Home?* I am a little bemused, trying to form my thoughts around the word.

We pull up in front of a familiar square white building. The wheelchair I am transferred to is new and smells strongly of polished leather. It has a raised and slightly curved head-holder that helps me hold my head straight. My head does loll sideways as the wheelchair is tilted to climb the one little step into the drawing room of our ground floor flat, but it stays straight once someone nudges it back in place into the holder. Suddenly, I feel a sense of relief and calm as I am wheeled inside – through the drawing room, into the dining area in the middle of the flat that opens onto the small berra, then briefly into a small bedroom on the right side. The familiarity of it all envelops me. The tension gripping my mind releases a little and I feel a sense of comfort. *Home!*

Until I get to my room. A single hospital bed has replaced the low double bed that I have always slept on. *Where is my bed?* My irrational mind wants to scream. Instead, my body shakes with tension. I feel myself being lifted out of the wheelchair and onto the new hospital bed. The mattress is strange, it seems to undulate for no reason. I protest in the only way I can, by flailing and thrashing my useless body. People scurry around me, everyone talking loudly. *I may not be able to move or speak, but I can still get a reaction.* This is my only thought as I fall into an exhausted stupor.

'Hey Ram, hey Ram.'

I wake up to the clatter of utensils in the kitchen and the sound of a familiar bhajan playing in the squat blue and silver Philips CD player next to my bed. My arms and legs hurt, and I feel a deep desire to stretch. Khushi seems to sense that I am awake. She is already bathed and changed, and has probably also done her morning puja since I can smell the agarbatti. She cranks up the bed a little, pausing every time she sees me wince. She wipes my face with a cool towel. My arms and legs, which have been trembling with their need to stretch, suddenly find release as she moves them gently back and forth and massages them. A teaspoon of bitter liquid is slowly poured down my throat.

'Antacid,' says Khushi, 'it will make you comfortable.'

One of the young men who was in the crowd of people milling around the house yesterday enters the room.

'Good morning, Sahib,' he says, his hands folded in a namaste. 'Ready for chai?'

He threads his hands under both my arms and pulls me up a little, then cranks up the bed until my back is almost straight. I feel myself helplessly tilt to the left, but a pillow is quickly wedged between my body and the bedrails. Khushi arrives with a mug full of steaming hot tea and a couple of Parle biscuits on a small plate. The young man tentatively tries to give me some tea with a spoon, but my teeth clatter uncontrollably, spilling most of it. Not a good idea. He then tries holding the mug to my mouth and I slurp some tea. This works a little better than the spoon. I still struggle to keep my lips puckered to avoid dribbling all the tea out, but we probably get fifty per cent of the tea in my mouth, interspersed with a few small bites of the biscuits. All this time, Khushi and the young man keep chatting. *Who is this boy*, I want to ask. *Please tell me what is going on.* But of course no words come out. I wait patiently till they realize that we need to be introduced. Finally, Khushi looks at me.

'This is Rajesh,' she says. 'He will be here with us every day to help you.'

'We need to find a good attendant, a responsible young man.' I had overheard Khushi chatting with Amiya at the hospital before we came home. The requirements were way beyond that, I knew. Someone who can be trusted with a person who is currently completely immobile and helpless. Someone who remembers the little things – that my muscles have weakened, that I bruise easily, that there is always a catheter hanging beside me that needs to be moved with me, and can never be yanked by accident. Someone who can sense my discomfort. Someone who will be comfortable with me, who can communicate with me, talk to me, not just attend to my needs mechanically.

Rajesh is about twenty-two years old and physically strong, which is a key requirement since I am hard to move. My bones are stiff, my muscles are immobile, my body is floppy. I am not that light. I weigh about 75 kg, or did a few months ago, not sure now. The leaden state of my body makes it harder to move me since I do not pull my own weight, even a little.

When I am shifted from the bed to the wheelchair, or vice versa, the person holding my shoulders has to be really strong. He leads the effort. He gets his arms under my armpits and gently locks his hands across my chest. He has to do it very carefully, because if he puts any pressure, he can injure me very easily. He coordinates with the person who's assisting, that is lifting the legs. 'Ready?' he says, and they both take a deep breath. 'One, two, three, go!' and they do. If they mess that up, it can be a disaster. It could be a fracture, or worse. Khushi tried to help a few times, with the legs, but even that is difficult for her. Every move has to be planned and scheduled, so that a second helper can be available for a few minutes to assist with the transfers at different times of the day.

I always liked routine, but now it becomes my lifeline. I am moved from the bed three times a day, the first one being what I call a triple transfer. The morning triple transfer starts around 8:30 a.m. after morning tea in bed. I am moved from the bed to my regular cushioned wheelchair, have breakfast at the dining table in the lobby, and then get horizontally shifted to a metallic bath wheelchair and wheeled into the bathroom for a shave and shower. I go back to my bedroom covered with a bathrobe. After a relaxing oil massage and dressed in a fresh set of clothes, I am back in bed for a short nap, partially reclined and propped up with pillows, usually facing the single small window in the bedroom.

The second transfer happens around 1:00 p.m. after my morning nap and glass of coconut water. I am fed lunch at the dining table in the lobby, after which Rajesh parks me in the drawing room while he goes and eats lunch. Khushi takes a short break after what is usually eight hours of non-stop activity, eating her lunch and watching *Balika Vadhu*. I try to show interest by staring intently at the TV for a few minutes, but the exhaustion of struggling through lunch and my complete lack of interest in the high-drama TV show overwhelms me as I doze off. Even if I am not tired, I close my eyes, partly to block out the shrill dialogue, and partly so that Khushi can assume I'm sleeping and watch without guilt or feeling the need to check on me. At 3 p.m., I am wheeled back to my room and settled back in bed for a horizontal afternoon siesta.

I wake up around 4 p.m. and get propped up for a cup of tea, followed by exercises. The third transfer of the day happens around 6:30 p.m. I 'eat' dinner at the dining table, and then get wheeled into the drawing room for TV time. Evening TV is more interesting than *Balika Vadhu* – usually the news, followed by some old Hindi film songs, and old British comedy re-runs. I hum along in my head to the lilting melodies and poetic lyrics of the 1950s, and laugh aloud at the antics of Mr Bean, my body shuddering with unexpelled laughter. Usually, Sowmya calls around this time. Rajesh leaves for home around 8:30 p.m. after transferring me back to bed for the night.

My basic routine is now ironed out. Morning tea. First transfer, the triple. Breakfast at table. Shower. Back in bed. Nap (on right side). Coconut water. Second transfer. Lunch at the table. TV. Back in bed. Nap (on left side). Evening tea. Exercises. Third transfer. Dinner. TV. Sowmya's daily call from Boston. Back to bed.

After a week, physical therapy gets added to the daily routine, after my evening cup of tea. Mr Joshi, the therapist, who lives in our neighbourhood, is an army man through and through. Even though he is retired and now freelances as a physiotherapist, his bearing is upright, his hair and moustache always neat and trimmed, his clothes impeccably ironed, his mannerisms calm and unruffled. He treats me with the deference he would show towards a senior officer in the army, always starting the conversation with a 'Good evening, sir'. There is a momentary pause, an imperceptible click to the heels and an invisible salute as he greets me, so ingrained in him after years in the army that he can't help it. Then, he starts chatting about this and that as 'we' exercise in a leisurely and unhurried way.

This is now becoming the best part of the day, seeing my limbs move. Despite Mr Joshi's subtle efforts to convince me that I am doing all the work and he is simply helping, I am well aware that my arms and legs are being moved for me. Still, it brings them alive for a while as I gaze at them nostalgically, dreaming of the days that they worked and trying to control the sense of anticipation that they will be working again soon. *Be patient, Raj – it takes time.* I also enjoy the social event that the physical therapy session has become. Mr Joshi, Rajesh, and Khushi are always there. Whoever is visiting at that time joins the session, offering their own words of encouragement and clapping, especially during the independent sit-up (or rather 'prop up and hope that he doesn't topple') and twisting moves.

One variation in my routine, depending on the weather,

has to do with going out. Even though windows stay open, Khushi wants to make sure I get some fresh air and sunlight. The first few days, Rajesh and Khushi include me in an errand to the *Mother Dairy* booth to pick up milk every morning. I do not enjoy that at all. I usually look down at my hands, trying to ignore the curious glances and stares all around me. Maybe my discomfiture is obvious, or maybe Khushi is concerned about the traffic and potholes on the road, but after a few days, we stop doing that. Much to my relief, going out now is just a quick stroll in the wheelchair either before breakfast or in the evening after tea, limited to maybe fifteen minutes, just a few turns on the small concrete area behind the flat, where we usually don't meet anyone.

Another variation is provided by visitors who drop in, of which there are a lot in the first few weeks of coming home. My durbar, Sowmya calls it in one of her phone calls. I smile at that, and imagine myself as an emperor – holding court, greeting visitors, noting their discomfiture, nodding briefly in acknowledgement but letting the lesser beings do all the talking and activity. There are usually two locations for my durbar. The first is me sitting up in my hospital bed, the catheter tube and bag discreetly covered with a sheet draped on my legs and hanging over the edge of the bed. The visitors are either sitting on the narrow divan facing my bed, where Khushi sleeps at night, or on plastic chairs pulled into the room. The second scenario is me sitting in my wheelchair in the drawing room, and everyone else on couches and armchairs that have now been pushed to the walls to make space for my wheelchair. In either situation, I am uncomfortable. I was never one to seek attention, and being at the centre of it, especially in my current state, is difficult. But I am also grateful to be part of life as it swirls around me, and not set aside.

Conversations usually start with visitors addressing me. 'How are you?' they ask, knowing very well that I can't respond but unsure of what else to do. Not quite sure how to handle the lack of response, everyone still feels compelled to start a conversation with me, to acknowledge me in some fashion. Khushi quickly answers on my behalf, with varying levels of detail, depending on the person and situation. After that initial interaction, the conversation flows across me, over me. I am there but not quite a part of it. Relieved at the dissipating attention, I nod off. Most visits are pleasant enough, not particularly helpful, but somewhat uplifting, and at the very least, not very annoying. Some visits, usually those that go on too long or that get into awkward, intrusive questions about how we 'manage' certain activities, make Khushi a little distressed and angry. But she shrugs it off.

My first real trip out happens two weeks after returning home. Khushi has been worried about the catheter and urine bag, and worried that the longer it stays, the more 'used to it' I will get. Nitin, her brother, has been calling around to get an appointment with a reputed urologist at

Gangaram Hospital, and we are going there today. The drive to Gangaram is loud and chatty. The drive back three hours later is quiet and tense. I am exhausted. I was wheeled around as we looked for the doctor's office, then waited for an hour in the narrow, gloomy, and crowded hospital corridor for our 10-minute audience with the famous doctor, who shook his head and firmly dashed everyone's hopes of the catheter being removed to the ground. 'The catheter is his best friend for now,' he said. *And forever* – I muttered in my head, filling in the blanks.

I am unable to sleep tonight. My bed is at a 30-degree angle. In the grey beam of moonlight filtering in through the window screen, I watch Khushi lying on the divan in a perfect shavasana. This is how she has slept every night for the past forty-four years, dropping off only when completely exhausted, into a deep, well-deserved slumber. I clamp my lips together as much as I can to quiet the cough I feel coming, knowing she will jump up at the smallest sound and start to scurry around. For a little bit, I just want to look.

6

Always the Better Half

'The Taurean female is the salt of the earth, a combination of most of the sterling qualities every male looks for and seldom finds. She will play the game of life fairly, with cool, admirable calm.'

– Linda Goodman

1965–1969

I closed my eyes and let the warm sea breeze sweep across my face, meandering through my wiry, close-cut hair and coaxing it up. After almost eight years in Britain, I was looking forward to going home. Not sure if it was my sense of adventure or a meek attempt to fulfil my desire to experience life at sea, I had decided to spend some of my savings and two weeks of my time on an ocean voyage aboard the *S. S. Chusan*, possibly the only one of my life. The wind on my face as I stood at the ship's bow was a reminder of my teenage dreams, but also brought relief at the realization of how far I had moved on. The sorrow, regret, and anger were gone. When I had gone to the UK,

I was fleeing the bonfire of my dreams. This, on the other hand, was a journey towards a new life, one I had worked hard for, and was truly excited about. The bright blue waters of the Mediterranean, the cultural melting pot of Port Said, the slow crawl through the Suez Canal, the pyramids. I filed away each visual memory, selectively asking someone to take a picture or two with the new camera I had bought myself as a going away gift. I arrived in Bombay a happy man, visited my parents for two weeks in Shankar, and then settled into a 24-hour train journey to Madras and my new life.

In Madras, I worked as an engineer in the quality control department at the new factory, a giant new modern facility that buzzed with excitement and throbbed with anticipation. I shared a nice, large flat with three friends, and lived an idyllic bachelor life. We lived like expats working in a developing country. We had a cook and a maid, went to the Club most evenings for a game of tennis or squash, and even bought a car – which was a big deal in those days. Living and working with very close friends made it one of the best periods in my life. The only thing I missed was my family. I worried about my parents getting old back in the village. The long train ride prevented me from seeing them often. But I could get to them when needed.

* * *

We were in Patiala at Chhote Chachaji's house. He had just come back from the ice factory. His wife, Sushma, had just set down a large steel oval platter piled with piping hot pakoras on the dining table which we were all sitting around at, and was dispersing large helpings on quarter plates around the table. Sushma, who was twenty years her husband's junior, had recently taken on the unenviable task of mothering Chhote Chachaji's five young daughters, the oldest of whom was only five years younger than her. On the day she walked into this household, she had decided that demureness was not going to help her accomplish this monumental parenting task. She abandoned the shy bride persona almost immediately, and now ran her household with the authority and confidence of a brigade commander.

Chhote Chachaji started talking about a friend who had suggested a match for me.

'I am not sure now is the right time,' I said hesitantly. I was feeling a little overwhelmed, having flown from Madras ten days ago to help Biraji, who needed emergency prostate surgery, and then somehow ending up 'seeing' a 'doctor girl' who happened to show up with my uncle while I was staying overnight in Delhi on my way to the village. I had just realized how awkward it is to say no after seeing someone, even if there is supposedly 'no pressure'.

'The girl has an M.A. in Sanskrit and is teaching at a college. Her father is an IAS officer. Good family.' Chachaji continued undeterred, and passed around a black-and-white picture. I took it casually, making sure I looked nonchalant and expressionless, and did not glance at it for too long, as is polite in such situations. Despite my best effort, I probably stared longer than was appropriate. In the picture, she sat on a stool in a photography studio, her brows slightly furrowed and almost connecting as she tried to tilt her face in the photographer's direction. A round, soft face, earnest and honest, a stubborn angle to the chin, the hair pulled back sternly and appearing again as a single braid resting on her shoulder. I did not object when a meeting was suggested.

* * *

I got up hurriedly from the couch when she walked in, looking tentatively around. She wore a grey sari with a patterned blouse, hair tied back neatly in a long braid that swung down her back nearly to her waist, small earrings, no makeup. No surprise there. In those days, makeup was worn by women who were frowned upon – actors, performers, forward young girls. She greeted all the elders respectfully, and then there was a bustle of activity and hurried movement as everyone arranged themselves appropriately, which somehow resulted in her sitting on the same couch as me, her eyes examining the intricate pattern of the Kashmiri rug in front of us, the middle cushion providing a respectable distance between us. There were murmurs of conversation as everyone tried gently to get comfortable.

'How was your drive to Patiala?' asked my uncle.

'Quite uneventful, thank you,' replied her father.

'At least the summer heat has subsided,' said my uncle.

They continued a slow, steady conversation, making sure there was no awkward silence as Khushi and I assessed each other, subtly. At some point, the older men decided to take a walk in the garden, leaving just the two of us sitting there, and Sushma Chachi bustled out to the kitchen muttering something about checking on how the tea was coming along, leaving just both of us in the room.

After a brief silence, I finally turned towards her, intending to ask the getting-to-know-you questions about her life, education, job, among others that I had prepared. Instead, I froze. I was suddenly struck by a moment of self-doubt as I stared at her flawless porcelain complexion.

'Would you be comfortable with my dark skin colour and the acne scars on my face?' I blurted, kicking myself as soon as the words escaped my mouth, embarrassed by the sheer foolishness of my opening remark. She looked confused, obviously unprepared for such a question, smiled, and nodded.

She told me later that she was expecting to be quizzed and assessed as a suitable bride, and she found it very touching that I even thought of her feelings. Plus, she added with a smile, she thought I looked like Rajendra Kumar, the actor, a flattering comparison indeed.

* * *

The baraat had reached Shimla at 4 p.m. that evening, a cold, foggy day, with the sun already setting behind the dark clouds, and had been welcomed at the guest house by Khushi's father Pitaji, all three of Khushi's young brothers, various cousins and uncles, plus a retinue of staff scurrying around, clearly outnumbering the twelve members of the baraat.

As was customary in those days, only men from my family had gone to Shimla for the wedding, while the women stayed behind to make arrangements back home for the bride's welcome. In some ways, the day when a son of the village got married was a day of uninhibited freedom for the women. With the men away, they emerged from the shadows, shrugged off their domestic burdens for a couple of days, laughed freely and loudly, lifted their veils, looked up and ran rather than forcing themselves into a slow, steady walk. They did not mind missing the actual wedding. They got a few days off, and entertained themselves with music and dance sessions that often carried on all night.

The other reason for the limited number of guests was Biraji's general reluctance to impose any burden on anyone, even though Pitaji had assured him that there would be no problem hosting a larger baraat.

I vividly remember our white wedding in Shimla. Three hours under a cold, starless sky, and a beautiful mandap made of flowers intricately threaded together and draped lovingly on a wooden frame, from 2 a.m. to 5 a.m. as per the muhurat. While most weddings see everyone wandering off in different directions as the ceremony proceeds, in this case, the warmth of the holy fire kept everyone huddled close. Khushi and I had blankets thrown on our shoulders at some point, probably when someone noticed my weak effort to stop my teeth from chattering, and her bright yellow sari-clad figure trembling gently. Endless cups of hot masala chai were accepted gratefully by the audience, including the priest. But there were no short cuts or inappropriate rush.

The enthusiastic congratulations and blessings that came with the final phera were definitely tinged with relief as we all made our way inside the house. It all felt unreal. Was I really going to spend the rest of my life with this girl? Would she really be like the person I had pieced together in my head, based mainly on my imagination, and a few nuggets from one meeting and six letters exchanged over the past three months, most of which had been factual accounts of her college and daily life, and, honestly, somewhat boring?

I needed to wait longer for answers, as my new family surrounded me. That Khushi was the eldest of nine siblings meant that I had a number of young faces looking at me, the younger ones staring at their first jija in an awestruck manner, the older ones, too mature to gawk, glancing periodically at me. Everyone sat around and introduced themselves, chatting away until Biji came and shooed everyone aside. Without even a word exchanged with my new wife – and not sure what it would have been anyway, I was whisked away to the guest house to get some rest before our trip back to Shankar later in the morning.

The sky was grey and overcast, as was the mood at the bride's house when we arrived there after breakfast. I was completely unprepared for this dramatic shift, from the joyous chatter of a few hours before to awkward goodbyes and tearful farewells. *I am not kidnapping her, and you will see her again*, is what I wanted to say, but instead mumbled something like, 'Thank you.'

'They are supposed to cry at the bidaai,' whispered Sukhdev encouragingly. 'She will be fine as soon as we leave.' He was wrong. The next few hours, once we got into the decorated car that proclaimed our special status as a newly married couple, consisted of me staring at the beautiful view as we drove down the curvy, mountainous road, while she looked intently at her knees all the way. She refused to get out of the car even when we stopped for a snack at Solan, a hilly little town that existed mainly due to its location halfway on the winding 5-hour road trip from the plains towards Shimla – once India's summer capital under British rule, its role as a mini-hub for local orchard farmers, and its proximity to a brewery set up by a local landowner. I periodically glanced at Khushi whenever I heard a choked sob, usually to see a tear drop into her lap or her hand impatiently rubbing her eyes to prevent one. I wanted to say something but was at a loss for words, and did not want to make anything worse.

Another sharp contrast hit me when we reached Shankar and the creaky wooden front door opened to a cacophony of excited female voices and a beaming Bhabho with an aarti thali, ready to welcome the newest member of the family. 'Look, Bhabho,' I teased my mother. 'You said no one would give their daughter to your dark son. I brought home the fairest bride in decades.' My fair bride's face looked more red than ivory under the gentle but direct scrutiny of the coterie of women welcoming her into her new home, as well as from my remark.

Her face remained flushed through the evening as I awkwardly untangled the symbolic knot on the kangna, and went beetroot red when she 'won' the icebreaker game that proclaimed her the dominant spouse in our relationship. The next couple of days were a blur of people visiting us, blessings received, and eating a never-ending stream of laddoos.

Khushi was beginning to converse, still quietly and hesitantly. She had started moving around the house comfortably, even remembering to cover her head when the male in-laws were around. She was talking and looking visibly relaxed when I gave her another opportunity to blush with embarrassment. My mother was asking if she should travel to Madras with us to help Khushi set up.

'No, leave us alone for six months,' I said. 'We need some time to get to know each other first.'

I moved my belongings from the bachelor flat to a breezy two-bedroom in Nungambakkam as Khushi and I started our new life, where the furniture ordered for us by Khushi's parents and shipped all the way from Panipat had already been delivered. She was getting more comfortable with me, still struggling with mixed emotions as she balanced the excitement of her new life with the sadness of leaving her family behind. I must admit I had very little patience for her 'family talk'. Perhaps it was just my ego that demanded her full attention, but I found it hard to focus on her rambling tales about her brothers and sisters. Khushi had a big family, each person seemed to have a lot going on, and they were all connected in a way that was unusual to me. To me, who had a healthy relationship with his brothers, but did not necessarily feel the need to connect with them deeply, I felt she was perhaps too involved with them. I wanted her to focus on her new life and not think about them all the time.

Long distance was still tolerable, since I was insulated and unaffected by the constant writing and reading of letters, but the chaos was inescapable when we went to visit them. There were so many of them, and when they were together, they all seemed to talk at the same time, expressing diverse opinions freely and loudly. With so many people involved, it was difficult to ever get anything done. 'Even planning a picnic is impossible in your family,' I remember saying uncharitably to Khushi, who, to her credit, usually did not respond to my jibes.

But we both always fulfilled our responsibilities to my family and to hers. One year after we got married, Biraji had a major setback, he couldn't walk properly and lost his memory. No one was quite sure what had happened, MRIs did not exist in those days and the general opinion was that perhaps he had a stroke. Khushi and I took a plane from Madras to Delhi, which was very expensive in those days, especially since we were still paying off our wedding debt. For a few days, I took care of him, carrying him on my back when we visited the doctor, until he got a little better and began to walk again. Khushi stayed with him for a month until he could care for himself, while I went back. When Biji and Pitaji came to visit us in Madras, I made sure I spent time with them, showing them around Madras, driving to Rameshwaram on a weekend, and generally being a good son-in-law.

Khushi was quickly assimilated into my close-knit group of friends, with the wives taking on her indoctrination into the basics of a corporate spouse's life in Madras; dealing with the heat and humidity, shopping, cooking, navigating through and managing domestic staff without knowing the local language, learning some basic Tamil – as well as the more interesting parts, driving and swimming lessons, the latest hairstyles and leggings, the mahjong club, wine-making. She tried a lot of new things, and I secretly hoped that she would get over her strict vegetarianism as she spent time doing cooking experiments with her new friends.

'Bought some chicken today on my way back from the factory, looks very fresh,' I said casually, putting down a package wrapped in newspaper and tied with string on the kitchen counter. 'Do you think you can make it on Saturday when the Bhatias come over?'

She did not respond for a few minutes, puttering around the kitchen, fussing over the tea-tray, arranging the matching tea-pot, milk-pot, sugar-container and cups, averting her eyes from the newspaper wrapped package on the counter that was already disintegrating in a pool of liquid.

'No,' she said flatly, just as I was getting my hopes up. 'Maybe you can drop it to their house to be cooked. And please drop it tonight if possible, otherwise I will not be able to open the fridge till it is gone.'

It was not going to happen. I gave up the thought of ever eating meat in my own house ever. I was doomed to be an 'outside non-vegetarian' forever.

Overall, it was a good life. Five sets of white shirts and white pants – perfect for the Madras weather and the unofficial uniform at the factory based on its overwhelming popularity. The 7 a.m. carpool ride to the factory. Driving one day a week with four pick-ups made it well worth being driven the other four days of the week, the lively quintet arriving at work refreshed after belting out the latest English and Hindi songs along the ride. The 7 p.m. gathering at the Madras Gymkhana – tennis or squash followed by a swim.

Weekend visits to the private beach where our wonderful MD graciously hosted all of us, lots of picnics during the relatively less warm winter months, weekend visits to Yelagiri to escape the stifling humidity during summer. Rowing matches, racing in 'teams' as we drove to weekend outings, constant rotating dinner get-togethers.

Laughter. Youthful energy. Hope and ambition. Work and personal life overlapped, but in a wonderful way. These were the people I worked with and played with, the people I understood and trusted. This was my extended family. My personal ambition and discipline, and my faith in these strong relationships kept me going as I decided to step outside my comfortable quality control lab and immerse myself in building an enviable distribution and service network for the company over the next 20 years.

Khushi and I were both responsible individuals who started our marriage with a serious commitment to each other. That commitment grew into a loving, comfortable, respectful, and trusting relationship. She watched out for my lack of focus in social situations. When I kept nodding and saying 'very good' to a friend's seven-year-old daughter who was sadly telling me she got zero on a test, she nudged me gently and responded with appropriate empathy on my behalf, giving the little girl a quick hug. When I serenaded Neeru with the song 'Mera Dar Khula Hai, Khula Hi Rahega, Tumhare Liye' while her husband snored through the movie we were all watching together, she smiled tolerantly, confident in our new relationship and completely understanding my sense of humour.

Khushi gave up her job as a college lecturer when we got married and moved to Madras, took a step down teaching at a high school for a few years when we moved to Calcutta later, but never went back to the college professor track. Her career faded into the background as we moved, dealt with family responsibilities, and welcomed Sowmya into our life. I have to admit that I showed little interest in finding out what she was passionate about, or supporting her in finding a way to resurrect her teaching career. I had a traditional, masculine, simplistic mindset. *Why would she work when she didn't need to?* In hindsight, I wanted to be the provider, and needed her to adapt to my ideal vision, picturing her enjoying a relaxed life made me feel good. I encouraged her to have fun – learn swimming, start driving, develop her own independent social life, go out with friends, play mahjong. Later in life I wished that I had not assumed I knew what was best for her, understood her passion for learning, and supported her in continuing her pursuit of academic excellence. But she never complained, and it honestly did not cross my mind.

7

The Sounds of Silence

'It is futile to hunt for joy and peace in the outer world.'

– Agastya Raj

July 2010

After the first stroke, I had lost function in my legs and one arm but I could still use my right arm, and I could talk. My voice was hoarse, but only because the feeding tube scraped the inside of my throat. My volume was low and my speech was slurred since my facial muscles were weak. My brain was a little confused initially, but the fuzziness cleared up in a few days. It was very hard to speak correctly and clearly, but the important thing is that I could talk.

I vividly remember my first encounter with a speech therapist. Till then, I had not even known that something called speech therapy existed. It was a couple of days after my first stroke. I was sitting up in bed, feeling somewhat happy that the feeding tube had been removed. Suddenly, the cubicle curtain whooshed open, and a young lady bustled in, holding a folder. She introduced herself quickly.

'My name is Anjana, and I am your speech therapist' and without a pause, continued, speaking slowly and loudly. 'Open your mouth and say "aaah".'

When I did, she continued giving me rapid orders to mouth different sounds. I followed her instructions initially, then got increasingly annoyed.

'I will see you tomorrow,' she said, after fifteen minutes, leaving as quickly as she arrived.

After that, whenever I saw her approach, I would close my eyes, look the other way and pretend to sleep. I managed to avoid her a few times with my little trick, but she would usually come back a few times and peek through the curtain until she caught me with my eyes open, and promptly start my 'speech therapy'. She always spoke loudly, in that slow, encouraging, childlike voice that teachers use with toddlers or native speakers use with foreigners. I would squeeze my eyes shut even more tightly. I would grit my teeth as she leaned close to my face, continuously telling me to repeat inane sounds after her. *I am not deaf or blind!* screamed my brain, desperately wanting to say something to her, but like many of us, I was hesitant to question medical professionals.

She was probably well-trained, but that might have been the problem. I think she had a step-by-step training manual on 'Speech Therapy after Stroke' that she had read once and applied to every patient. She arrived, implemented her lesson, and checked me off as a job well done. She made no effort to ask who I was, how I was doing, feeling, or really understand what state I was in. Not once did she try to communicate with me in a normal fashion. If she had, she may have discovered that I could actually talk, although in a hoarse and hesitant voice!

When you lose your physical ability and feel vulnerable, the tone a person uses takes on even more importance. Anjana's tone, lack of respect, and condescension were infuriating. I did not want to say 'aaah'. I did not want to make that sound because it made me feel stupid. After a week, I became completely resistant. Whenever she showed up, I would just close my eyes tightly even if they had been open, not worrying any more about my displeasure being obvious, and not respond at all when she addressed me. Even though I did not say anything to anyone, Khushi and the nurses could now tell that I was not enjoying my speech therapy.

One day, Khushi hesitatingly told my neurologist during rounds – 'I don't know what the problem is, but he is not participating in his speech therapy. Is there any other speech therapist who we could try?'

Soon after I moved to Heritage Ward, I was informed that the 'senior' therapist was going to take over my case. Coincidentally, like my physiotherapist at home later, his name was also Mr Joshi. He was a pleasant and welcome surprise. A gentleman with all the signs of approaching middle age – a slight stoop to the shoulders, sparse grey hair, a range of smile and frown lines beginning to get etched permanently on his face, a wispy moustache, along with a soft voice and soothing manner that belies the general image of the loud Punjabi. He looked me in the eyes, smiled, shook my hand like a gentleman, pulled up a chair close to my bed in order to hear my hoarse whispery voice, and to my surprise, actually had a conversation with me. He had obviously read up all the notes about me. But the only time I was reminded that he was there as a therapist was when he gently made me repeat a few words that I had mumbled during our conversation. He didn't make me say 'ah', 'bah', 'ga', and other nonsensical sounds.

I began to look forward to his daily visits. He was less like a therapist and more like a pleasant visitor, with some therapy thrown in. Mr Joshi's visits were abruptly brought to an end when I ended up back in the CCU after my second stroke and doctors were too busy dealing with more complicated medical issues and getting me to a point of stability. The second stroke, as you know, led to an entirely different universe of problems.

I lost all movement from the neck down. I could move my head, I could create expressions with my face, but from the neck down I was almost completely lifeless. My head was full of cement, and my body had become infused with heavy metal. The doctors tweaked my fingers and toes, prodded my limbs, tapped my joints to see a reflexive response, hoping for a little bit of movement, but there was really nothing there anymore.

I had also now lost my voice completely. Not gradually, but all at once. I couldn't even say 'aaah' anymore. If I tried really hard, the best I could manage was a strange hissing sound, or a very disturbing guttural growl. I remember overhearing the doctor tell Sowmya, 'Just imagine that there's a dictionary in his head and it's been wiped out.' That was very accurate – it was like the place in my head that held my dictionary had been disabled. I had no words. I had my vocal cords, I had the ability to create sound, but I didn't have any words.

When you can't speak or move, it's hard to acknowledge that you have heard and confirm what you have understood, and impossible to let others know what you think. I had no mechanism to communicate. Not only could I not talk, I also couldn't gesture, write, or draw.

Biji has come from Shimla to visit me. Despite her best efforts, tears liberally flow down the wrinkled contours on her weathered 90-year-old face as she holds my limp hand in hers, rubbing it gently as she tries to transfer some life energy into the floppy appendage. Khushi had told her about my condition on the phone, but I guess she was still not prepared to see her son-in-law in this state.

'Why not me?' she cries softly, 'It's my turn, not yours.'

I continue to stare mutely at her while my eyes cloud over. *I'm okay*, I try to say, but what I hear is a hoarse moan that I do not even realize is coming from me until she looks up at me expectantly, hoping for more.

I am definitely not going to try to say anything else, if this is what my throat is transmitting. Instead, I try to nod and wait patiently till Khushi scurries in with a cup of tea and escorts Biji to the divan.

Uma bhabhi is sitting in my room drinking tea while I try to eat the digestive biscuit that Rajesh has dipped in tea and is holding up to my mouth. Uma is visiting from London, and has landed a few hours ago at Delhi airport. She will stay with us for a couple of days before her brother picks her up and drives her to her family home in Punjab. She seems to be staring very intently at the cup of tea in their hands, savouring every sip. The chair she is sitting on is placed at an angle to my bed, one that allows me to see the person without turning my neck too much. Uma can look at me directly, but her eyes seem to shift away every time I try to make eye contact and communicate my questions.

I have noticed that people seem to find it hard to meet my gaze in general. I'm not sure if they're uncomfortable looking at a completely paralysed body, or at the pipe that constantly drips urine into the bag hanging by my side. This is quite ironic, since the only possible way I can communicate anything is through my eyes. Whenever they divert their eyes, my head screams, *I need you to look at me!*

Uma seems even more uncomfortable than most of my other visitors, and almost determined not to make eye contact, even by accident. The conversation meanders on her plans to visit the State Bank of India in Janpath in the morning to close an account, besan barfi, her plans to stay for a month in Punjab. Since I cannot ask, I wait for a mention of Baldev and some explanation of his absence, but there is none. So I draw my own conclusions.

* * *

Two months after coming home, I see Mr Joshi, the speech therapist hovering near the door to my room.

'I am sorry I did not call,' he says hesitantly, 'I got your address from the hospital and decided to stop by today since I was visiting friends in the area.'

I am happy to see him. It has been over three months since he last worked with me. I have a lot to share with him, but can only smile my welcome. He makes small talk about the weather and tells me how stressed he is about his son's Class 10 Board Exam. I stare at him intently, hope rising and almost choking me with excitement, swallowing frequently, wondering if I should try and say something. My unasked question hovers between us.

Do you have a magic formula that will bring my voice and words back? Meanwhile, while we are working on that, do you have any non-verbal communication tips that I can use to ask the hundreds of questions and dispense the thousands of responses that circle around in my mind, constantly fluttering impatiently until they drift away and collapse with exhaustion? I am now trembling in anticipation, my limbs going rigid in a pleasant spasm. But he doesn't move beyond the small talk.

When Mr Joshi gets up to leave, I hear Sowmya having a long conversation with him outside my room. They speak in low tones. I cannot hear the words. Her expression is blank and downcast when she turns back and heads to her room on the other side of the dining area. After a few minutes, she returns to my room, the smile back on her face.

'Mr Joshi is going to stop by every few weeks, whenever he has time from his busy schedule at the hospital,' she says, still sticking with the 'everything will be all right' theme and attitude that has been established in the house. I shake my head gently, seeing right through her words.

Tell me the truth! screams my brain. *I am quite sure he will not, since there is no point. There is only so much even a knight in shining armour can do.* I think back to the last time I spoke actual words to my daughter, over the phone, when she was leaving for Boston. 'I will miss you,' I had said. I wish I had known at that moment that it was going to be the last time that I would speak to her verbally, ever. There is so much more I could have said.

Mr Joshi's visit might have seemed like a glimmer of possibility, but has merely served to puncture the protective layer of denial we are wrapped in and confirmed what we already know but are finding hard to accept. My word dictionary has been completely wiped from my brain. I will not speak again. Once it sinks in, I go numb for a few seconds. Then a general sense of calm overwhelms me as I let go of the possibility.

* * *

A few days later, Khushi comes bustling into the drawing room where I am sitting in the wheelchair before dinner, looking quite excited. She makes an announcement.

'I know you are having trouble talking, but we can read something together.'

I wince a little bit as she clumsily puts my reading glasses on my nose. I twitch my nose to nudge the glasses into the right place. She places a newspaper on my lap with a flourish, and pulls up a stool next to me. I look down expectantly, staring at the squiggly black shapes dancing on the paper, blinking my eyes as I wait for them to clear into images I can recognize. Nothing happens. I continue to see a sprinkling of black on white, with no idea about what I am supposed to do. Khushi sees me staring straight at the newspaper.

'Are you reading?' she asks, gently at first. 'Take your time. Let me hold it up for you.'

She falls silent and watches my eyes continue to look at the newspaper. She looks increasingly concerned as she moves and adjusts the newspaper and then, getting slightly agitated, starts to move my head from left to right. I can tell from the increasing tension in her touch and voice that she is getting worried. But she controls herself, casually folds the newspaper and puts it back on the coffee table.

'He does not want to read just now,' she explains to Rajesh, 'he must be tired.'

Thereby they maintain the myth, or at least pretend to do so for my benefit. Meanwhile, my ears started humming with a strange sound, almost as if they are trying to drown out the infallible truth. I have lost all my words, spoken and written. I have no words left at all.

8

Rise Above Not-So-Petty Things

'Frame your life with faith.'

– Thomas Monson

1977–1982

I had very little patience with religion for the first forty plus years of my life. In my youth, I only saw the rote and ritualistic side of religion – going to the temple, sitting there quietly, mumbling bhajans, eating prasad. As a child, I participated in the bare minimum of family pujas, only showing up when someone noticed that I was missing, found me and ordered me to join. I usually sat there, sullen, with my eyes downcast, my hands in my lap, mouthing the prayers and aarti I resisted learning, running back to my room as soon as prasad was distributed.

There were also some incidents of open rebellion, when even quiet acquiescence was beyond me. One morning, when I was about twelve years old, Bhabho told me to matha teko in the small mandir at home before I left for an exam.

'I have studied,' I said belligerently, 'I don't rely on god, good luck, or good fortune to do well.'

Seeing her shocked expression at my outrageous statement, I dragged myself unwillingly to the mandir. But as soon as her back was turned, I left my chappal right next to the puja thali in front of the kuldevi, and headed to the exam determined to do well and prove the disconnect between prayers and personal success. My experiment with logic was however, to the rest of the family, not just disrespectful, but an enormous act of defiance, and sacrilege, and neither were acceptable.

When I got home from school, I headed straight up to my room above the guest room as usual, but was almost immediately summoned to the main baithak.

'BHIGA'! It was the loudest and firmest voice I had ever heard.

Could that be Biraji? Sounds like him, I thought in the few seconds it took me to process the very different, firm, and angry undertone to his usually soft, quiet way of speaking. I headed down quickly to find Chachaji sitting on the divan, his back straight, a firm look on his face. My legs shook as I stood there, *a petty criminal summoned to the king's court.*

'Bhiga, your mother tells me that you left your chappal in the mandir. Is that true?'

It was posed as a question, but not stated as such. I nodded imperceptibly, unsure about whether to speak, and also unsure about whether my vocal chords would function under such stress. I stared at my feet quietly, willing my knees to stop trembling, waiting for what came next.

'Please go take a bath and clean the mandir. And this will never happen again.'

I let out a deep breath, relieved at the relatively mild sentence, and hurried back to my room. After that, Biraji and Chachaji never mentioned it again, but Bhabho could not get over the incident. She did not speak to me for days, leaving the room abruptly when she saw me, shaking her head and muttering something, with the word 'nastik' somehow always audible. My emerging desire to express my opinion about life and religion diminished significantly. I remained a closet atheist, but kept my thoughts to myself. In an odd way, that incident was the foundation of my firm belief that one's beliefs and values are deeply personal, and best kept to oneself.

The next time I went over the line was when I was in college. Meat of any kind or eggs had never crossed the threshold of our Brahmin threshold, and the thought of anyone ever touching meat was inconceivable. A friend from college who was visiting and eating dinner with us accidentally mentioned how much I enjoyed the meat samosas in the hostel canteen at Hoshiarpur. The family erupted in horror.

Biraji, always the conflict avoider, immediately left for a walk. Bhabho declared me a confirmed cannibal, and spent many days shaking her head and sharing her shock with her coterie of friends and followers. 'It was to be expected,' she would say, pausing for effect, 'from a boy who never prayed properly in the temple. Did I ever tell you about the day he left his shoes in front of the kuldevi when I told him to offer a prayer on his way to his exam. Can you believe what he said – "I will not bribe god with a laddoo",' she continued, paraphrasing my statement from six years ago.

* * *

Khushi had been brought up in a family where everyone knew their aarti, participated in a havan on each person's birthday and observed basic customs around fasting, praying, and special food on days like Janamashtami and Shivratri. After we got married, I continued to participate in family prayers at home, grudgingly and minimally, folding my hands and accepting prasad, but not really paying attention, and watching Khushi's earnest devotion in a fond but distant way, unable to relate to it, but willing to accept it.

The Jagannath temple in Puri is famous as one of the Char Dhams, and also for the Rath Yatra. It was the dramatic descriptions of the relentless unstoppable rath in this annual event that morphed into the English word 'juggernaut'. A couple of years after getting married, Khushi and I visited Puri. While going somewhere to see god (*Isn't god supposed to be omnipresent?*) was not something that made sense to me, I was interested in trips to famous holy sites not as a pilgrim, but as a tourist. I enjoyed the art, architecture, the stories, the symbolism, and the rich history associated with old holy sites. When we reached the Lingaraj temple area, we spent some time exploring.

'It's time for evening darshan,' said Khushi excitedly around 5 p.m., scurrying towards and quickly blending into the swarm of humans that was morphing into a rough line outside the main temple. I stared at the line ahead of us in dismay.

'I am not sure I want to stand in queue to see god, or rather an image representing god,' I said, expressing my thought louder than I realized. Khushi's face went red with embarrassment as the lady ahead of us looked back with a shocked expression on her face.

'It's only going to be about twenty minutes,' she pleaded quietly. 'We can't turn back from the temple dwar, it's bad luck.'

But I had already stepped out of the line and was headed to the beach, my feet sinking into the blissful sand, my mind focused on picking the best spot for watching the sun rise the next morning. A very mortified Khushi trailed behind me, uncomfortable with the idea of not waiting for darshan, muttering a prayer, probably seeking forgiveness for both of us.

Many years later, when we travelled to Calcutta and toured the eastern part of the country in 1994, I insisted on taking Khushi to the Lingaraj temple, this time doing full darshan. I am not sure I made up for the trauma I had caused her many years ago, but I tried.

When we lived in Calcutta in the 1970s, Khushi decided to fast on Mondays. In those days, the three of us would leave home together in the morning, and I would drop Sowmya and her to their respective schools before heading to work. Every Monday, she would want to stop at a small roadside Shiva temple on the way. And every Monday, I would get annoyed. But she would still ask every week, hopefully.

'It will only take a few minutes,' she would say.

I would park near the temple and wait – 'You can go if you want to.'

And I would stay in the car with Sowmya, impatiently tapping the door handle.

I never tried to influence Sowmya with my views on religion. In fact, I never discussed it. For me, beliefs were very personal. Khushi would sometimes say I should talk to Sowmya more about what's right and what's wrong, concerned that we were not providing her a religious foundation she could relate to later in life. My response was always the same – 'Everyone learns from their own experience in life.'

* * *

After my father died in 1978, I found myself becoming more introspective, more aware of my mortality, and the mortality of those I loved. We moved back to Delhi in 1980, a move that I had advocated for, since it put me closer to Punjab and Bhabho. Rents had skyrocketed in the few years we had been away in Calcutta, and the best we could afford in the familiar neighbourhoods of South Delhi seemed to be tiny, claustrophobic DDA flats. Having an open space to escape to was important to me, and basking in the winter sun was Bhabho's favourite pastime. After much deliberation, we rented a house in a slightly distant neighbourhood in West Delhi, one with a full terrace, and settled in. Unfortunately, Bhabho was able to enjoy our proximity and the chhat of our house in West Delhi for only one winter. She passed away within a few months of our move.

Losing both parents hit me hard. In my mid-forties, I felt strangely orphaned. I took another final journey to Haridwar with her cremated ashes. I had done the same a few years earlier, but this time, I felt the emotions more deeply. As I released her ashes into the holy waters to merge with nature and be one with the universe again, something stirred in me. The symbolic process of letting go of someone who has passed on, freeing them from the bondage of life, to explore the universe as a free spirit, was so final, so beautiful, so peaceful. Walking through the small galis to our family pandit's library and signing the scroll he carefully rolled out for me, and reading the names of many ancestors going back 150 years ago made me reflect on things I had not given much thought to – human life, existence, cessation, continuity.

The loss of my parents did not immediately direct me towards religion and spirituality, but it probably created a vacuum, one that stretched into a gaping hole when I signed the sale papers and handed over the keys for Pande Nivas to a complete stranger, racked by guilt at my inability to afford the upkeep of the home where generations of my family had lived. My roots had now definitively been sliced off, or so it felt at the time.

The change in my attitude started happening gradually after I went with a friend to listen to a talk by Swami Chinmayananda, a Hindu spiritual leader and teacher who was known for taking the core of the Bhagavad Gita and Upanishads from the original Sanskrit that very few people could access or understand to everyone through simple lectures in English and other spoken Indian languages. He believed that Hindu religion as practised had become superficial and ritualistic, and had embarked on a mission to bring the wisdom and teachings embedded in ancient texts to everyone in a relatable way. Like many others, I was not aware of the treasure-trove of deep thought and philosophy in the old scriptures that underlay the tangible practice of religion. Swamiji had studied the scriptures for many years in Rishikesh, observed the disconnect between thought and practice, and decided to make it his life's mission to bring the scriptures to the people, help them apply these thoughts to their daily lives, and return Hinduism to its fundamental belief system.

The Hindu religion has many facets and variations, but its core philosophy is a belief that god is present in everyone, that we are all one with the universe, and part of a universal life force. The goal of religious or spiritual practice is self-awareness and self-discovery. Hinduism is more about self-development, turning inward to improve oneself and increasing our capacity to help others. It is about a personal journey that brings forth the concept of self-improvement through exploring and understanding oneself from philosophy to practice.

For me, this was a very different perspective on religion, one that completely resonated with me. Khushi and I became regular attendees at Chinmaya Mission discussions and discourses. Very often, Swamiji would conduct a multi-day workshop around one chapter of the Gita, translating and focusing on the thoughts embodied in each verse. The discussions were stimulating, humorous, never boring. The examples were real and relatable. There was no preaching, no commands, no rules, just exploration of thought. Attending lectures, reading Swamiji's books, and listening to recordings became a key part of my daily routine, even more so when I retired.

How much did it change me? Did I become a better person in any way? Did I evolve into a stronger human being? Or was it just academically interesting stuff that made me feel good? Now that I have lost my ability to read, speak, or discuss anything, I have the opportunity to apply everything I have read and learnt, become mentally tough enough to take life as it is, through faith and spirituality. May god give me strength.

9

The Centerpiece

'Learn to live with your loneliness creatively.'

– Agastya Raj

October 2010

The mountain has come to Mohammed today. 'Namaste.' The usual greetings happen all around as Deepti's future in-laws trickle in, everyone edging around each other and adjusting into the limited space in the drawing room. Deepti is Khushi's niece, Nitin's daughter. She is ten years younger than Sowmya. I have watched her grow up since we moved to Delhi, and we have remained close. She has always been very fond and respectful of me, and spoils me, and even now, never forgets to bring back my favourite lemon tarts any time she goes to Connaught Place.

Today, she is getting engaged. The engagement party is not very formal, there is no pandit or religious ceremony, just the families getting together, exchanging greetings, and blessing the couple. I am touched that Deepti has insisted on my participation in this important life event, and as a sign of respect, brought the venue to me. She probably never thought her engagement would be in a home filled with medical equipment, centred around an immobile man in a wheelchair in the very narrow drawing room, only about fifteen feet wide and twenty feet long, with barely a foot of space on either side between my wheelchair and the sofas against the wall for people to sidle through. I mentally hunch my shoulders as people brush past me. I feel uncomfortable, in the way, impeding the flow of people and refreshments.

I need to look relaxed and happy, I tell myself sternly.

It is a quiet event, nothing dramatic. I feel awkward that everyone has to interact with me, and that everyone's deference to me adds a touch of solemnity to a joyous event. Also, while I am used to a few visitors, this is overwhelming for me. In the midst of so many people for the first time, I feel like a stage prop that someone forgot to move before the curtain rose.

I am also tired. The whole day has been chaotic, with the bell and phone ringing continuously and everyone running around to get organized. I have done nothing to help of course, but I am exhausted and have a throbbing headache. I am trying to keep my eyes open to signal my involvement. I try to look as positive and attentive as possible when I am greeted, but am relieved as the focus shifts away from me. I watch the conversation quietly, and gaze at the dhokla and imarti being passed around with cups of tea. I have already eaten in my room, private dining being a preferred option in my state. Deepti and her fiancé exchange rings amidst applause.

Jitey raho, I mentally raise my hand to their heads as they bow before me.

Amiya is scurrying around as usual, looking tired but happy. *How quickly time flies*, I think. *Nitin and Amiya were just kids when Khushi and I got married; now they're in their 50s and Nitin's daughter is about to be married.*

My mind drifts back to our wedding for a second, Amiya's sweet and innocent face in a red wool knit cap and Nitin's mischievous young grin next to hers – too manly at age nine to wear a cap. I vividly remember their excitement when they visited us in Madras for their summer holidays, their awestruck faces when they first saw the ocean at Marina Beach, their amazement at the tropical heat and humidity they had never experienced growing up in Himachal, how impressed they were with their older sister for getting married and going to live somewhere so exotic and different from the small towns amidst snowy mountains they were accustomed to. Later, Amiya also stayed with us in Calcutta in 1977 for a few months, where she was doing research for her Ph.D.

She now lives in an apartment that is exactly a two-minute

walk from ours. When she moved there with her husband Devender, Khushi and I were happy that we would see more of her. We assumed we would continue forever our pleasant tea get-togethers and conversations about everything, from politics to cricket, from music to jokes. After Sowmya moved to Boston, Amiya would joke with me.

'I have a double role in your life, right Jijaji? I'm subbing for Sowmya too!'

But the joke about subbing for Sowmya has turned a little bit serious now. Instead of just subbing, Amiya has become the central pillar of Khushi's support system, her first responder, the first person she calls for all the little and not-so-little crises she faces every day, whenever she needs advice or just someone to keep me company while she takes her monthly trip to the bank.

* * *

'How are you doing, Papa?'

I have just finished my evening tea and am sitting in my wheelchair in the drawing room when Sowmya calls from Boston. Rajesh is holding the phone to my ear as Sowmya updates me about her children Rahul and Atul, and tells me everything that has happened the day before. The only sound I can manage is 'mmmm'. A guttural sound. Encouraged by this audible response of sorts, she rambles on, trying to make her monologue sound like a conversation.

'What do you think?' she asks me. 'You would like that, wouldn't you?'

I try to form sounds with my mouth in response, unsuccessful after that first effort.

'I hope you did your exercises,' Sowmya ends cheerfully. 'Make sure you do as much as you can. I'll come and see you soon.'

'He tried to smile as you were talking to him,' Khushi, who has been sitting next to me quietly and watching me when I am on the phone, tells Sowmya later, filling in the gaps by describing my side of the 'conversation'.

My attention varies during these phone calls. Some days I am engaged, my face trembling with effort, sweat meandering down the channels on my face, as I try to emit a sound, any sound. Other days, I am totally exhausted, and just sit in my chair totally blank while Sowmya chats on the phone. She can't really tell, and keeps going.

My eyes suddenly pop open. It is quiet, except for a soft hissing sound from the air mattress that undulates gently beneath me. It is dark, but my eyes focus on a very familiar silhouette looking at me. I smile broadly and close my eyes as Sowmya reaches down to give me a hug. I take a deep happy breath, enjoying this pleasant dream.

'Good morning, Papa,' says Sowmya cheerfully.

She is actually here! – my heart leaps with joy.

She has flown in from Boston the night before, and is now seated on Khushi's bed across from me, eating her favourite breakfast – gobhi paratha with dahi. I know that every two months, Sowmya takes off three weeks from work to be with me, but someone has removed the cardboard prop-up calendar that used to be next to my bed, probably to make space for the black medicine case and other assorted items, and I am losing track of dates.

Good, that way, I get a surprise!

Sowmya is chatting with Khushi – upcoming appointments, medicines, other potential visitors. She calls Amiya to announce her arrival: 'I'm subbing for you now,' she says, 'take a break.'

For the few weeks that Sowmya is here, I can sense that Khushi worries less. Even though Rajesh is there every day, and she trusts him completely, she always wants to make sure that there is someone else around, in case he needs help, or has a sudden question, or god forbid, there is an emergency. While she has led by example to make sure someone is always watching me, she knows that it is easy for my attendant's attention shift to a phone call or a video game. She rarely goes anywhere, and if she needs to go to the bank or some other errand, Amiya usually comes over. And Khushi always rushes home as soon as she can.

While Sowmya is here, she has a more relaxed morning – she can take a longer bath, not rush through her morning prayer, watch a TV serial at a volume level she can hear the dialogue at without worrying about missing any signal of discomfort from me.

I shake my head at the ongoing humorous banter about Team Raj, with Khushi as the captain, and their jokes about substitutes. I appreciate how my family has kept life normal for me in a very abnormal situation, how they centre their conversations and activities around me, or drag my wheelchair to wherever the action is. Never for a moment do they make me feel less relevant or respected. They never avoid eye contact or physical proximity. I can sense that they are doing this without seeming to focus all their attention on me, but it is clear that their attention never leaves me.

'He's going to get better soon,' is the thought I hear most often, stated and unstated, in conversations, over the phone, wrapped in every hug, suspended in the cloud of positive energy hanging in the room, entwined in the informal circle of support surrounding me.

'Yeah, maybe next year we can take a trip to the golf club, get back on the practice range.'

Khushi always has an upbeat tone, and everybody else follows her lead. Everybody wants to believe it. And I need to believe it, if I am to ever emerge from this physical prison.

Like everyone, I have my good days, medium days, and bad days. On bad days, I feel totally out of it and can't open my eyes. I don't want to interact with anyone. On medium days, I will open my eyes a little bit, kind of ready to tolerate the day. On good days, my eyes light up and dart around, interested and almost looking forward to my morning tea. These differences are not obvious, but Khushi senses them, responding with even higher levels of enthusiasm and chatter on bad days.

When I wake up the next morning, Sowmya is sitting next to my bed, waiting for me to stir.

'We are trying something new today,' she says.

After my shower and breakfast, instead of the nap I am looking forward to, I am wheeled into the drawing room. The bell rings at 11 a.m., and to my surprise, Mr Joshi, my physiotherapist appears.

Aren't you supposed to be here in the evening? – I wonder.

'We are going to try some tilt table exercises today,' says Mr Joshi, sounding excited, pointing to the long, narrow cushioned platform that has been placed against the wall.

It looks like a narrow massage table with straps for my body and little plastic cups at one end to hold my feet so that I won't slide off.

'The table will help limit the effects of immobility, improve bone density, cardiopulmonary function, and gastrointestinal motility, reduce pain, and improve your recovery,' he continues, getting a little technical as he expectantly sets up the table.

And then, what? – I wonder.

Under Mr Joshi's direction, I am shifted to the 'table' and belted in securely. Rajesh cranks a lever at the base, and the table is gradually raised, pausing every ten degrees to 'check in with me', which really means staring at my face for any sign of discomfort. Soon, we are at a seventy-five-degree angle. I have not been this close to vertical for a very long time. My head feels strangely light and I shut my eyes to ignore the dizziness. My feet throb with anticipation as the blood rushes to them, then start quivering, surprised, as they adjust to supporting my weight. I feel very nervous, almost more helpless than usual, if that was even possible, propped up, almost standing while having no control of my limbs.

'Okay, you're standing now. How does it feel?' says Sowmya, almost shouting excitedly.

I try to control my sense of panic, and close my eyes to shut out the swirling room.

The rest of the day, thankfully, is the same as usual. Lunch, rest, tea, TV. I watch very intently today, since there is a cricket match, pushing the table-top feeling to the back of my mind. I enjoy watching cricket, tennis, or old Indian music shows. I cannot watch new movies, talk shows or soap operas. I like to hum along in my head to the golden oldies on MTV, but cannot focus when the latest Top 50 start playing. When I am not interested, my eyes close, I relax my neck, and drift off to sleep. As soon as someone notices, they switch the channel to something else they think I will like, gently shaking me to draw my attention back to the TV.

Someone will always sit with me while I watch. Quite often, one of my arms will slide off, and hang limply for a few seconds until someone places it back on the armrest. Sometimes my foot will slide off the foot rest, and again wait patiently to be put back. Everyone is very careful about my TV preferences. No one changes the channel randomly when I am watching. It's almost amusing.

Sometimes, Khushi will say, 'Okay, you watched a long time. Can I watch my show for a little bit?'

It's not like I can say anything in return. Even Rajesh has learned to do that.

He will say, 'Sahib, can we watch Taarak Mehta for some time?'

As if I can say yes or no. They could turn the channel to whatever channel or programme they want. Yet, even though I have no control over the situation, they are polite enough to ask. To change the channel without asking me indicates that I don't exist, don't matter or have finally become invisible. It is a symbol of respect, an acknowledgement of my existence as a person, with thoughts and preferences. And it means a lot to me.

For no particular reason, my lips quiver and I feel a tear sliding down my cheek. *Is this how I am going to spend my final years, in this limited state? Do they really think I am going to get better? We talk about a lot of things — food, the news, the weather, an upcoming cricket match. But is there something we never talk about? Are the conversations in the other room different from what I hear? What is it that no one ever says in my presence?*

Khushi dries my face and gives me a hug.

'Come on,' she says to me, 'what do you want to do?', while looking around for something to distract me. 'We didn't read the newspaper today,' she says brightly. On other days, she may say, 'Let's put some music on. Do you want to listen to this?' Or, if Sowmya is in Boston, she will glance at her watch and say, 'It's almost time for Sowmya's call.' Something random. And my tears will usually stop, but my sadness doesn't quite go away.

10

The Arrival

'It's the courage to raise a child that makes you a father.'

– Barack Obama

1970–1991

September 1970. A Monday. I was just finishing a cup of steaming hot tea after coming home from work when Bhabho came scurrying in from the balcony of our first-floor home in Safdarjang Enclave. 'I think we have visitors,' she said. 'It must be Sohan.' Sohan is Uma Bhabhi's brother, who had recently completed his residency in London, and was moving back home to Jalandhar to start his medical practice.

Bhabho rushed inside to change her 'home' sari into a 'visitor' sari, one that had been carefully ironed and was hanging patiently in her cupboard, waiting for her next visitor. Bhabho was seventy-five now, but extremely particular, with simple but strict rules. One of which was to never be seen by visitors in crumpled clothes. Khushi scurried to open the door as the bell rang. As she opened it, I heard a strange sound. *Sounds like a baby*, I thought, puzzled. *That's odd.* The sound grew louder as I got up and joined her at the door.

It was definitely a baby, wailing loudly now. Sohan was standing outside, holding a carry-cot in one hand and balancing a large shoulder bag on the other shoulder. In the carry-cot was a baby, who looked about four to five months old, wearing a one-piece suit made of towelled cotton, feet kicking furiously, arms raised, wrists clenched, eyes squeezed shut, face red with effort as she powered her screams.

'Here she is,' Sohan announced, as he handed the carry-cot to Khushi and the bag to me, sighing with relief.

While Bhabho and I stared dumbfounded, Khushi showed her usual presence of mind. She scooped up the little girl, took her to the bedroom for a wash and change, and then quickly rummaged through the bag to find a carton of milk formula and a baby bottle. Within ten minutes, she came back with the baby in her arms, calmly sucking at the bottle. Meanwhile, Bhabho and I were still standing at the door, blankly staring even forgetting to usher Sohan inside for the mandatory cup of tea. I realized he had been talking but I had missed most of it.

'Come in, Sohan,' said Khushi.

'Sorry, Bhabhi. I need to get back to the airport to clear

my medical equipment through Customs before they close. I just wanted to drop Sowmya off first. I will stop by tomorrow,' he replied.

Before we could gather our thoughts, he had already said a hurried goodbye and left. That the baby had a name was all I got from the conversation. Tucked in the carry-cot, there was a note that referenced a letter, one that we had clearly not yet received. The note had detailed instructions on Sowmya's general routine, and eating and sleeping habits. But no explanation for her arrival, since that was in the missing letter that was probably still lying in a box at a post office somewhere.

Bhabho had received a telegram from Baldev in May announcing Sowmya's birth in London, and laddoos had been distributed throughout the village to celebrate the arrival of a new grandchild. She had booked a call to share the news with us. Khushi and I had been very pleased to hear about the new baby and had written a congratulatory letter to Baldev and Uma, asking when they were planning to visit India (they had not been able to travel back home since their marriage three years ago), and adding that we were looking forward to meeting their little girl.

Now, suddenly, the little girl was staring at us as she sucked vigorously at the bottle. This was not how any of us had envisioned our first meeting with Sowmya. Nor could anyone at that moment have foretold how significant this day would be in our lives.

I watched Khushi happily playing with the new baby, having completely forgotten about dinner, which would normally have been her entire focus at this time of the evening. After about half an hour, she remembered.

'Can you hold her for a bit?' she asked, placing the baby in my arms and scurrying off to the kitchen.

Sometimes you don't know what you've been missing in life until you actually experience it. It wasn't as if Khushi and I were unhappy not having a child and desperate to become parents. A couple of years after we got married, relatives had started dropping broad hints about having children. Another couple of years later, the curious questions about our childless state had petered out as people either wondered privately if something was wrong, or just didn't want to hurt our feelings.

'I need to do something,' I thought as I stared at Sowmya, who I had hurriedly laid down on the sofa next to me when she started wriggling, worried I might drop her if she moved. 'I need to let Baldev know of her safe arrival.'

We headed out to Palam Airport, the only place where one could send a telegram after 5 p.m. When I came outside after sending it off, Sowmya was lying on the bonnet of the car with Khushi hovering over her. Sowmya heard my voice, looked up at me, and smiled. My heart melted in a peculiar way that I didn't quite think was possible. As I picked her up to put her in

Khushi's lap, there was an unexpected sense of joy, a sense of calm, and fulfilment.

On Wednesday, the letter arrived and brought some clarity. Baldev and Uma were both working long hours and lived in a London flat that did not permit children. There were constant arguments with the landlady, who had told them they would have to move by end-October. They were frantically looking for a house in a good neighbourhood where they could raise a family, but hadn't found one they liked and could afford. They had decided to send Sowmya to India for a few months to be taken care of by Jhaiji, Uma's mother, in Amritsar. Since Sohan was flying back to Delhi, they hurriedly got a passport and bought a ticket for Sowmya. We were now supposed to call Bhabhi's mother in Amritsar, so that she could come and pick her up in a few days. Once Uma and Baldev were settled in a new home and found a good crèche that could take Sowmya during the day, they would take her back to London. Meanwhile, they thought it would be best for Sowmya to be with family, even if family was over 4,000 miles away. Seemed like a logical plan.

We booked a trunk call to Amritsar. Since mail delivery there took a couple of days longer, they had not yet received the corresponding letter from London yet. Jhaiji sounded flustered and confused, and somewhat hesitant. She was already taking care of another grandchild and was a little unsure about taking on responsibility for another baby. 'I will call you back tomorrow,' she said.

Bhabho, sensing the difficult situation Jhaiji was in, immediately decided that it was her duty to step in, and volunteered to take Sowmya back to Shankar with her. She got very excited, and started making plans, thrilled at the opportunity to show off her third grandchild, eleven years and twenty-two years after the others. I was a little tentative about my parents taking on a five-month-old in their seventies but resisted an urge to get involved, reminding myself that it was probably none of my business.

'Are you sure?' I asked.

'Of course we are sure. It will give us something to do,' said Bhabho, brushing me aside. 'Call Jhaiji and tell her not to worry, we will take care of Sowmya till she goes back to London. Invite them to come and see her in Shankar when they can.'

After a few novel days with a baby in the house, we drove Biraji, Bhabho, and Sowmya to the railway station, got them settled into their seats on the train, and returned home, to a house that suddenly seemed too quiet. I was taken aback at the strange emptiness I felt. *Could a little person be in a house for a few days and create such a presence that her departure left such a giant vacuum?*

After a couple of weeks, I had a trip planned to visit our dealer network in Haryana and Punjab, and planned to stop by Shankar on the way back. Khushi decided to come along, looking forward to spending another day or two with Sowmya. We reached Shankar late on a dull October evening to find a very harried old couple struggling to take care of a little girl. Their initial bravado and excitement had given way to exhaustion, as the many sleepless nights spent as protectors of the precious amaanat had sapped their strength. Since this was a 'foreign' grandchild, they would not let anyone else from the village take care of her. They had been taking turns feeding her, changing her, walking around with her. Staying awake at night to make sure she was alright under the small net cover placed on her to protect her from mosquitoes. Worrying so much about keeping her safe and healthy that they had not taken her out of the front room since her arrival, afraid that she'd catch a cold from the gentle breeze that wafted through the berra. Basically, they were overwhelmed.

Khushi and I were shocked, and concerned. The next morning, we gently suggested that it might be a good idea for us to take Sowmya back to Delhi.

'For a few days,' I assured them, 'Khushi is home during the day and can take care of her.'

We braced ourselves for comments about our lack of experience, and our need for parental training, but there were none. My parents were relieved, knowing it was for the best.

Our lives changed dramatically as we adjusted happily to a young child. There was a flurry of shopping as we explored a new world of baby stuff – clothes, bottles, and toys. I discovered the joy of coming home to a house filled with the sounds of a happy baby every evening, automatically glancing up as soon as I got out of the car, expectantly scanning the first floor balcony for a little face peering down through the iron rails, looking forward to our daily car ride after dinner as Sowmya enjoyed her evening bottle of milk, engrossed in the landscape of cars, rickshaws, two-wheelers, lights, and the bustle of people scurrying around on the roads. Khushi was now completely immersed in the joys of parenting, with any thoughts of potential teaching jobs happily relegated to the backburner, for later. We knew this was a temporary gift, and kept reminding ourselves that Sowmya was with us for only a few months, but there are no halfway measures in loving a child.

Our little flying angel became a mini-celebrity. Our landlady, who lived on the ground floor, had four teenage boys and always longed for a little girl. She was overjoyed at the new arrival. Khushi and Sowmya spent some time downstairs almost every day, as the landlady was always finding a reason to have them visit. Khushi's parents were very excited by their first grandchild experience, and her siblings decided they needed to spoil Sowmya completely, competing with each other for her affection and keeping track of how many smiles she bestowed on each of them.

As the months went by, we didn't hear much from Uma and Baldev about their plans. We wrote letters every week, sharing detailed updates on Sowmya – her first tooth, first word, first sit-up, first crawl across the room. We were afraid to ask about their plans, concerned that asking the question might make them think we were getting tired of taking care of their child, and petrified that a question from us could set into motion events to send her back that we would regret. We were happy to enjoy the time fate had allotted us with Sowmya. We were just going to enjoy our temporary parenthood, for as long as we could. And we definitely weren't going to hasten anything.

One year became two, two years became three, then four. Her return to London was never discussed. Baldev knew that Sowmya was well settled with us, that she was happy, and seemed hesitant to disrupt her, knowing that if she went back to London she would be in daycare. What he was not considering was the emotional connection that was being created in Delhi, something that could not be broken at will. And honestly, Khushi and I weren't focused on what they were thinking, just happy to keep parenting.

I am not sure when we first started introducing her as our child. Maybe it was when we stopped correcting the natural assumption that people made. When we hired a maid to help take care of Sowmya and were concerned that she would not be fully invested if she thought the baby's parents were far away. The day I walked into the local store and didn't correct the shopkeeper when he said, 'What a wonderful daughter you have', when she carefully picked up something that had fallen on the floor and placed it back on the counter. Or the day we registered her for nursery school and added our names in the parents' section. *Why would we not? –* I remember thinking defensively. *Baldev and Uma are not here. Are we going to send her report cards to London to be signed?*

Baldev and Uma never mentioned taking Sowmya back to London but neither did they broach a conversation about her staying with us. The fact that they could decide to take her back at any moment was like a Damocles' sword that always hung over us. Conflicting thoughts swirled back and forth in our minds, between bringing her up as our child, reminding ourselves that we did not have the right to do so, and worrying about what would happen if something went wrong. Silently, we lived with the unspoken fear that our family could be pulled apart at any moment. Whenever we forgot that sword hanging above us, we were suddenly reminded of it. During trips back to Shankar where neighbours exclaimed about her resemblance to Baldev. The doctor forms where we hesitantly added our names as parents, and answered questions about family history. Our mute avoidance of Sowmya's sudden ordinary and innocent questions about where she was born.

'I remember exactly when I met you,' she said one day, looking up from her alphabet practice sheet. I stiffened for a moment. She stood up, on her imaginary storytelling grandstand.

'I was driving around with God in his car, in the front

seat,' she looking pointedly at us, checking to make sure she had our full attention. 'We were driving all day, looking for some good parents for me. But I did not like anyone I saw. We were tired and planning to go back to heaven when suddenly I said "Stop – I think I see them". She paused for dramatic effect. 'God rolled down his window and said, "Excuse me, are you looking for a little daughter?" You both smiled and nodded, and we all went home.' I clapped and gave her a big hug, amused at the creative thinking behind the story (there was some logic to it – how else would you find your parents besides driving around?) and relieved at not having to come up with an answer.

Sowmya was quite happy with her story, especially since it had been validated by our whole-hearted acceptance. It was told and re-told on many occasions, always generating much applause. And we were glad she had answered her own questions. How would we answer them? And, how would she react to our answers?

* * *

When Sowmya was five, Baldev and Uma had a son named Varun. Soon after, they came to India to visit, and we all went to Punjab together. Sowmya was a little confused by our insistence on addressing Baldev and Uma as Daddy and Mummy, but complied. We had always made her draw pictures and write letters to them regularly, and she, in her childish innocence, had never questioned it, accepting it as a sign of respect for my older brother, and the explanation that we were all one family.

We first went to Amritsar, where Bhabhi's family organized a formal havan recognizing Khushi and me as Sowmya's parents. I was completely overwhelmed, overcome with a strange mix of happiness, relief, and gratitude. After that, we all headed to Shankar to spend time with Biraji and Bhabho. I had brought along my prized possession – my camera, safely tucked into its special moulded brown case. The day after we arrived, we all headed up to the terrace to take family pictures. After taking pictures with our parents, we decided to take pictures of each family unit. When we were setting up their photos, Baldev asked Sowmya to sit with them. Sowmya glanced at me, and I nodded. She shrugged, went and sat down between Baldev and Bhabhi, and grinned broadly. A second photo was taken of Khushi and me. Somewhat belatedly, Baldev asked Sowmya and Varun to pose with us too. I did not say anything, brushing aside the incident. But clearly, Baldev had not given up his sense of ownership over Sowmya, I thought with dismay. The havan was nice, but it did not erase reality, or make anything more certain.

A few years later, Baldev visited us in Calcutta. A couple of days after he arrived, we were eating lunch, laughing and chatting. He was trying to engage Sowmya in conversation and, like a normal eight-year-old, she was happily discussing the latest Enid Blyton book she had read.

'And do you know where you were born?' Baldev suddenly asked, casually.

'Safdarjang Hospital in Delhi,' replied Sowmya confidently, much to our surprise, stating a conclusion she had apparently reached on her own once she outgrew the transfer-from-god's-car story, I presumed. Khushi glanced at me, suddenly worried about the intent look on Baldev's face and the direction the conversation was taking.

'No, you were born in London,' he stated flatly.

'No, I was not,' said Sowmya, laughing triumphantly and quickly correcting his statement. 'Mama and Papa have never lived in London.' Brother clearly could not help himself at this point.

'That's because Mummy and I are your real parents.'

Sowmya started to smile, looking around the table, expecting to see everyone laugh at the joke. Confronted by silence and averted eyes, her eyes swivelled to me, boring into mine with laser sharp focus, expecting me to challenge the statement. My heart was thudding loudly in my ears. I could not trust myself to speak. I said nothing. The small smile on her face vanished. She looked confused for a few seconds, and then a blank, expressionless mask dropped on her face. She stood up and walked out of the room. It was the first time ever that my daughter, who loved rajma-chawal, left the dining table in the middle of a meal.

I was too much of a coward to follow and talk to her, my ability to deal with emotion being as stunted as it had always been. When upset, I always withdrew into a shell. And I was unable to say anything to Baldev. After all, it was true. I was overcome by a cloying and oppressive combination of respect for my older sibling, gratitude for the gift of Sowmya, helplessly confused about where his rights ended and mine began, feelings that seemed to outweigh my gut desire to protest his words and protect my daughter. So I did not reach out to comfort her.

Khushi rose from the table and went off in search of Sowmya. Later, she told me what happened. Sowmya was sitting quietly on her bed. When Khushi entered, she asked just one basic question:

'Are you my parents or not?' She clearly expected, and desperately needed, a black-and-white answer.

'Yes, of course we are,' said Khushi, sitting down and grasping Sowmya's hands in hers.

And that was it. Sowmya didn't speak to Baldev during the rest of his stay, and the topic never came up again.

* * *

'I won all the class prizes – except sports, of course,' said Sowmya, grinning as usual. It had been a few months since Baldev's visit. Since the day he threw a bombshell at the dining table, I had been worried about the impact on

Sowmya. I heaved a sigh of relief – all was well with our child, I told myself.

Life went on in its neat rhythm. Sowmya was a good student, an easy child, happy to spend hours absorbed in her books. Sports and physical activity, however, were not her comfort zone. She was hesitant to roll down the little hills of Nehru Park at age three, tentative about jumping in a pool at age six, and unsure about riding a bike even at age nine, despite my best efforts to encourage a sense of adventure in her. Her lack of interest in sports was puzzling to me, and a little disappointing, but I finally put away any thoughts of playing a game of tennis or racing a bike with my little girl, and learnt to enjoy her as she was.

Work was busy and challenging as I built and grew the dealer network across the eastern part of the country. The post-colonial lifestyle was alive and well in Calcutta in the 1970s. I enjoyed my 5 a.m. golf on weekdays, alternating between the RCGC and Tollygunge Club. More leisurely games on weekends were often followed by a nice fish and chips lunch and a cold beer in the Tollygunge clubhouse. Non-golf weekends were not so bad, either, it just meant spending more time in the Tollygunge pool with Sowmya and Khushi. Weekday evenings often included a short trip to the RCGC Annexe in the Maidan area, technically for lawn bowling on the little remnant of British India it represented, but more for the hot shami kebabs, samosas, and the toothy welcome and friendly chatter from the Bara

Chokra and Chota Chokra, the custodian of the bowling green and his successor.

Visiting new places was an added bonus with a sales-related job for someone who loved to travel. Khushi and Sowmya would often accompany me on trips that happened during school breaks. We went to Assam, Meghalaya, and Bhutan during my stint in the eastern region. Later, we travelled to Punjab, Rajasthan, and Himachal Pradesh together.

* * *

The next shock came out of the blue when Sowmya was fourteen, in the form of a rare phone call from Baldev. We exchanged letters frequently, but international calls were still expensive and sparingly used in the early 80s, so it had to be important.

'We were thinking that it might be a good idea for Sowmya to continue her education in London', he said casually, after exchanging pleasantries.

'Well, I don't know if she will adjust to a different school system,' I replied lamely after a short pause, weighing my words carefully, my hand beginning to sweat profusely as I clenched the phone, that strange mix of respect and gratitude once again choking my natural response. 'She's a very good student, always ranked first in class, and I am not sure we should disrupt anything.'

'Well, in that case, you don't want to hold her back, do

you? We all want to make sure we provide all the exposure and opportunities for her, right?' he said, latching onto my comment. 'Why don't you send her for summer holidays here?' he continued.

'Yes, of course,' I mumbled quietly.

Khushi was quite upset with me for entertaining this proposal, but I convinced her that it may be a good idea, and we should not let our selfishness stand in the way of Sowmya's future, reminding her once more of our unending gratitude to Baldev and Bhabhi. Over dinner, we broached the idea with Sowmya.

'What about visiting Daddy and Mummy in London this summer? It will be a fun trip. And you can also visit some high schools to see if you want to study there. Good students like you often go abroad to study,' I said.

Her initial excitement evaporated immediately when she learnt we were not planning to go with her.

'I don't want to go by myself. Why can't you go with me?' she said, getting increasingly annoyed when I kept persuading her. 'Why are you forcing me? Why don't you just say no? We can all go together some time later,' she said, with a finality that indicated that the topic was resolved for now.

She was somewhat bemused and suspicious of our efforts to persuade her to go, not understanding why she was being shipped off to a holiday abroad on her own. Then, she started getting really upset.

'Why can't you book a call and just tell Daddy that Sowmya is not comfortable travelling by herself,' she said, getting rather frustrated at our insistence.

But I knew my brother would be angry if we didn't send her. And one doesn't disobey an older brother, especially when one is the youngest in the family. So, we kept talking about the vacation till Sowmya gave up arguing and agreed.

We put on a brave face over the next few weeks, trying to get Sowmya excited about the trip, buying new clothes, figuring out what to pack, constantly telling ourselves that it would be selfish to stop her from exploring opportunities. At the airport, when we dropped her off with big smiles pasted on our faces, she looked at me squarely and said definitively, 'I will see you in four weeks.'

I nodded, trying to avoid thinking about her being gone forever. As soon as she walked through airport security, the smile I had pasted on my face vanished, my shoulders drooped, and a sense of loss enveloped me, roaring through my ears dismissing all the airport sounds around me, and then a suffocating silence descended on me as I drove back home. Even though neither of us mentioned it, Khushi and I knew there was a chance that she wouldn't come back at all.

There were many nights when I couldn't sleep, tossing and turning. Even with Khushi right there, the house felt terribly vacant. Every time the phone rang, I walked to it slowly, thinking this might be the dreaded call from Baldev letting us know that Sowmya had decided to stay there. I imagined Sowmya's voice on the phone, breathless with excitement at the new world she was discovering – *Papa, it is so nice here. There is a park in front of the house. It's not hot and sweaty. The school building is so nice, and the principal was so warm and welcoming.* I told myself, and strictly, *I am going to be happy for her, proud of her, support what's best for her.* The sword of Damocles was now dangling by a very weak thread, inching down, tickling my neck and the uncertainty tormented me.

Despite Baldev and Bhabhi's efforts to entertain her and convince her to visit schools there, Sowmya came back in four weeks as scheduled, with the same stubborn look she had left with, and a victorious twinkle in her eye. Baldev was a little unhappy when I called to let him know that Sowmya had arrived safely.

'She is a little spoilt, isn't she?' he said. 'Very stubborn. She refused to visit the school or meet any kids her age. And she can be a little rude, sometimes. When I mentioned that we would have never sent her to India if we had been able to buy the house we live in a year earlier, do you know what she said?' he spluttered, indignantly. 'She said – "I am so glad you did not". Can you believe that?'

I didn't respond, worried that he would hear the cheer in my voice at her response.

Sowmya had simply decided she wasn't going to like living in London even before getting there, and while she was there, she incessantly talked about going home. They took her to tour London, watch *The Mousetrap*, visit the Lake District. They cooked everything she liked to eat, and lots of new things for her to try. They visited family and friends.

But it was too late. There was absolutely nothing they could do to change her mind. For too long, India had been her home, we had been her parents, and there was no way to erase fourteen years of her life, and start afresh. I understood what had happened, but didn't think I could explain it to him without getting him more upset. So I apologized, saying something vague about talking to Sowmya and being stricter with her, masking the happiness in my voice with a serious overtone, and hurriedly put the phone down.

The year Sowmya went to London and determinedly came back home, we were dealing with a second downsizing event since we moved to Delhi. Our joy at owning our first home was overshadowed by the fact that it was a 'compact' two-bedroom flat, and it was on the ground floor, quite overwhelmed by the somewhat larger footprint of the flats above. The chhat was gone. *'Had I known I would eventually move into a flat anyway, I might not have pooh-poohed the idea when we moved to Delhi. But there is no choice now,'* I muttered to myself.

As usual, Khushi dealt with it better than I did, setting things up, figuring out a new maid, getting to know the neighbours as people moved into the newly built flats. It took me a while to settle in, with one major irritant. Since there was a long wait-time for phones to be installed, Khushi had generously shared our phone number with neighbours, for emergency use. Unfortunately, we quickly became the colony phone, as neighbours near and far generously shared our number with their extended families, none of whom hesitated to call at odd times, expecting us to call their kin for a long chat which, to my annoyance, never seemed as urgent as we had been earnestly told.

Sowmya did not miss a step as we moved from our old, rambling house in Kolkata to the modest rented home in Delhi, and finally settled into our cozy little flat. Along her journey, she skipped Class 4, moved to the more competitive environment at DPS in Class 8, studied Economics in college, and won admission to a couple of the country's best business schools.

We continued to enjoy our dinner table conversations and evenly split rotis, late night halwa whipped up by Khushi on demand, and played evenly matched games of Scrabble. Music was a big part of our evenings. My pride and joy was a beautiful wooden radiogram, a full console that had a radio on one side and record player on the other, with a classy tilted door, and neat drawers for my set of records at the bottom. By the time we settled into our flat in Delhi, it became much easier to use the radio/CD player, and the radiogram retreated into the storeroom. Mostly, we just sat around listening to and singing along to Vividh Bharati. Sometimes, I would pull out the mouth organ that had been with me since I had bought it for myself in the UK. Sowmya would open up the harmonium she had acquired as we experimented with various Hindi film music tunes.

There were no tantrums, and rarely any demands or complaints. Besides books, there was very little Sowmya was interested in buying. Even though she had been chauffeured to and from school since she started nursery school, she patiently took local buses to college. Even after she learnt how to drive the large Ambassador around, there was never a request to take the car anywhere. It was a quiet, peaceful existence. We were happy, with no clouds on the horizon.

11

Circle of Love

'What I need now is a thrust in living, not retirement.'

– Agastya Raj

August 2010

It is going to be a hot and humid day. Early in the morning, I can feel the sweat tickling my legs through my thin cotton shorts and forming damp spots on my back. I wait patiently – not a choice, it's just that I have no way of showing impatience – distracting my thoughts from the discomfort by focusing on the bhajans playing on the CD player and humming along loudly in my head. Until I hear very familiar, boyish voices. *Am I hallucinating again?*

I see two smaller faces quietly peering at me.

'Is he awake?' one asks in hushed tones.

'Not yet,' whispers Khushi, 'let's go wash our hands and eat something.'

I keep my eyes forced shut, totally unprepared to meet my grandsons.

They saw me for a few minutes in April at the hospital, still and silent, strung up to monitors and tubes. At that time, they looked nervous and confused – awestruck and overwhelmed by the sights and sounds of the ICU. Now, it seems that they are back. *They are probably here expecting things to be back to normal, now that I am home and they have been told over the last couple of months that I am 'relatively better'. Rahul is eleven years old and Atul is almost ten – I'm not sure they understand that 'relatively better' does not always mean back to normal.*

I hear the excitement in their voices as they peer at me. I keep my eyes determinedly shut. *Are they expecting me to get up and play with them, go outside for a hose-pipe shower, maybe set up a game of chess, and referee their arguments like I used to do? How will they react to a grandfather who is stiff, immovable, and mute? Will they stare at me in wonder? Will there be temporary fascination followed by boredom? Will they walk away from me in disgust?*

Khushi has noticed my eyes flickering and gets going with the morning stuff – opening the small window to let in some light, cranking up the bed, dissolving that awful antacid in a teaspoon of water and putting it in my mouth, and turning off the bhajan as the sounds of real life take over. The boys come back in with Sowmya as I am being served my morning tea.

'Surprise!' they all say, as they gather around the bed. 'We are going to stay here for a month!'

Luckily, I don't have to try to look surprised; there is no point, no one would be able to tell. Inside, my mind continues to teem with conflicting emotions. I am overjoyed at seeing the boys again after having given up on ever doing so. I think that I would have thought twice before bringing them to what has by now become a mini-nursing home, and exposing them to the sordid side of old age. I would understand if their parents hesitated to do so, and decided to keep them away. I am deeply saddened at my inability to reach out and give them a hug. And I am acutely embarrassed, wondering what they think of the urine dripping into a bag suspended by my side, the biscuit crumbs all over my chest, the drool collecting at the corner of my mouth and my stiff, floppy body sprawled awkwardly on the bed.

Within moments, all the doubts swirling through my mind have vanished. I am enveloped in a bear hug as the boys climb onto my bed from both sides. Atul immediately turns to Rajesh, who is standing there with a cup of tea in one hand and a biscuit in the other, looking amused.

'I can feed Nana the biscuit,' he says confidently, immediately grabbing it before anyone has a chance to respond. I nervously watch the biscuit approaching my mouth, faster than usual, propelled by over-eager young hands.

Control, I tell myself. *Just the mouth,* I scream, as I feel my body tense into a potential spasm. I manage to take a bite without too much dribbling or spillage. I relax, assuming that Atul will now hand the biscuit back to Rajesh. But he doesn't. He sits there patiently, waits until I finish chewing, and then offers me another bite. His gaze is quiet and curious as his big brown eyes stare into mine. He is a little bit tentative, but positive and encouraging. Once I finish the biscuit, he jumps off the bed and joins Rahul on Khushi's divan-bed. I refocus my attention on the conversation around me – the flight from Boston, the weather, Sharman.

My new helpers decide to take an active role in my 'management'. Rajesh gets a break from feeding me breakfast – Atul manages the bowl of cereal and Rahul usually handles the toast. I join them for lunch and dinner, my wheelchair being rolled to the head of the table for each meal. After two to three days of watching Khushi or Rajesh coax small pieces of roti, softened with dal and sabzi, into my mouth at dinner, Atul decides that he can do better at the more complex challenge of managing my dinner. He puts his careful observation into practice, making right sized pieces of roti, alternately adding a dash of dal or sabzi, offering a teaspoon of yogurt after every four or five morsels to charge it up, taking small breaks when he sees my face and upper body shaking from the effort of eating.

Within a couple of days, my embarrassment fades completely,

replaced with a sense of gratitude for their immediate and absolute acceptance of the new normal. I stop pondering the irony of them taking care of me, when just a few years ago, I was feeding them dinner and wiping their drool. I have an even more overwhelming desire to hug them.

Every morning, I am greeted with bright young voices as they assist with my warm-up exercises, their gentle young hands massaging my arms and legs to reduce the overnight stiffness, before taking turns to crank up the bed. After my morning tea and biscuits, they drink their Bournvita milk sitting on Khushi's bed, followed by dalia or omelettes for breakfast.

'It's table time, Nana.' For the more hopeful, including the boys, the table is a magic contraption that represents an intermediate step towards beginning to walk again.

'See, you can stand!' they say encouragingly, glancing periodically from the Tom and Jerry show they are watching on TV. My mind flashes back, hearing the same words in my own voice, when Atul tentatively pulled his 11-month-old body up for the first time, staring at me with amazement as his chubby legs shook before he collapsed on the carpet.

The boys decide they need to improve my entertainment activity options. Maybe they sense my disappointment at the wooden alphabets I am asked to manoeuvre into slots on the board, or the chalkboard where my hand is driven to draw inane objects. On one of their outings, they pick up a couple of games that they decide to 'play with Nana'. One that excites them is called Rush Hour – it's a small, square grid where four trucks and about a dozen other cars of various sizes are stuck in a traffic jam, and the objective is to get your car through the gridlock.

One evening when Rajesh is off, the bed is cranked up fully and the game is set up on a pillow placed on my lap. With two other pillows on each side to prop me up, and the boys perched on either side of the bed, we are ready to play.

'What's your first move, Nana?' asks Atul. 'The blue truck should move up a notch, right? I saw you looking at it. I can help you with that.'

Rahul wants to help my hand make the next move. 'I think he wants to move the green car down now,' he says, following my gaze.

'No, he thinks he should move the red car next to it,' counters Atul. They argue about my next move until Rahul grabs my hand and does the move.

'See, I told you he wants to move the green car,' he says victoriously.

The humour of the situation fast overwhelms the irony, as Sowmya and Khushi start laughing. Soon, I am so involved that I feel like I'm actually playing. A surge of joy courses through me as my car escapes the gridlock and my grandsons slap my back joyfully. They continue to play until they realize how far down I have slid into the bed. There is a flurry of activity as everyone gets on either side to heave me back up, then promptly return to the game.

* * *

Today, I have not seen the boys all day. 'They went out for lunch with their Dada–Dadi,' says Khushi, guessing the question in my head as I stare at her intently. The day seems longer than usual. I have just finished evening tea in my room when the bell rings loudly and continuously. Atul enters the room, wearing a golden mukut and playing a wooden flute, perfectly angled, followed by Rahul.

'Happy birthday, little Krishna,' says Khushi, giving him a hug, getting misty-eyed as she remembers his birth on Janamashtami ten years ago.

'Let's go for the party, Nana,' says Rahul, quickly pushing down the brake and wheeling me to the dining table where a cake is waiting amidst a riot of streamers. Our very own Krishna beams happily as he cuts his cake, and we celebrate.

August goes by in a flash. Suddenly, it's their last day with us. It's almost 10 p.m. It has been over an hour since I was transferred back to my bed, and I have been watching the boys play a board game on Khushi's bed as Sowmya and I listen to some old songs playing on the radio. I am tired after all the excitement, but also hope no one notices the time. I don't want to give up yet. But Sowmya notices me slipping. As soon as she gets up and starts fussing around, the boys jump up.

'My turn!' they both cry out, grabbing the bar at the same time to crank down the bed. They both help with the night arrangement, pushing me onto my right side for the first few hours of the night, adding Pillow 1 under my head, Pillow 2 under my right arm, Pillow 3 between my legs, and Pillows 4 and 5 behind my back to make sure I don't flop over on my back. Sometime later, Khushi will remove Pillows 4 and 5, roll me over on my left side and mirror the arrangement.

'Good night, Nana. We have to leave early tomorrow morning,' they say as they give me a farewell hug. I drift into slumber. *God bless them.*

12

Going Global, Not by Choice

'A baby has a way of making a man out of his father,
and a boy out of his grandfather.'

– Angie Papadakis

1995–2004

My mind drifts back to the day our family triangle was startled by a new entrant and gently nudged into a square. I remember it quite clearly.

The quiet bustle of activity in the Park Hotel coffee shop. Khushi and Sowmya were sitting on the semi-circular couch while I sat on one of the two chairs across the table, my chair slightly angled. I looked pensively at the empty chair next to me, casting periodic glances through the strategically placed artificial palm trees that separated the coffee shop from the hustle and bustle of the hotel lobby.

'He's here,' Sowmya said in a quiet, flat voice. He noticed us and was heading in our direction as I stood up to shake hands. My first impression of Sharman – tall, painfully thin, quiet, thoughtful. Not sure what I had imagined, but I think I had built a larger-than-life image that needed to quickly adapt to the reality in front of me, and was relieved by it. All my apprehensions melted away as we painstakingly plodded through a conversation that was clearly difficult for all, once the initial questions about where he lived, worked, and the auto-rickshaw ride to Park Hotel were done.

'I just wanted to meet you,' I said lamely, not exactly elaborating on why. Sharman nodded and looked on, not quite sure what to do with the awkward pause that followed.

Khushi chimed in hurriedly. 'What's your favourite food?'

I rolled my eyes at her innocuous effort to keep the conversation going. Even though the question seemed more appropriate for a five-year old, it helped break the ice. We laughed for the first time with the young man who would even out our odd-numbered family and play such a large role in our lives. Very few words may have been exchanged, but a sense of mutual trust was established. And so we went from three to four.

Sowmya and Sharman were married in 1996. We spent the next year getting used to her living in another home in Delhi. In 1998, Khushi and I were caught up in the excitement around Sowmya's pregnancy. Sharman was away for much of the time in the U.S., attending graduate school in Boston and earning his M.S. in Finance. While he was away, the family cocooned around Sowmya. She was sent off to work with a whole basket full of food every day – a morning snack in a little plastic container, lunch in a three-tier, temperature-controlled tiffin, an afternoon snack in a container slightly larger than the one with the morning snack (just in case she got delayed at work), and a bottle of water (in case she got thirsty while in the car coming home). In anticipation of the arrival of a grandchild, sheets were embroidered around the edges, a special squishy pillow and swaddler were bought, and bright yellow sweater with matching cap and booties were knitted.

Early one morning in December, Sharman, who had just returned from Boston, called.

'We are leaving for the hospital' was all he needed to say.

We swallowed our morning tea, scurried around to get ready, and arrived there within an hour. It was a long day of pacing around and anxious waiting. We shared a tiffin lunch that Sharman's parents had brought over and ate chhole bhature from a fast food place for dinner, interspersed with little plastic cups of tea or coffee from the Nescafe vending machine in the hospital lobby.

By 10 p.m. I was tired and went home to sleep. At 11:30 p.m. the phone rang with the announcement of Rahul's arrival. The next morning, I was at the hospital at 8 a.m., waiting outside the nursery door for my first glimpse of the scrunched-up little face of my first grandchild. I remember smiling continuously all morning after that. Back home, we called everyone we could think of to share the news.

All my dreams of watching Rahul grow up over the next few years were sharply interrupted with a jolt a few months later when Sowmya casually announced, 'Sharman got a good job in Boston, with the money management firm where he was interning. Rahul and I might move there to join him.'

I knew I should have been happy for them, but it was hard to force a smile on my face when my heart was screaming, '*Nooooo! Don't take Rahul away from us!*'

'If we move,' Sowmya continued firmly, 'I want you to come and spend time with us.'

'Yes, of course,' I nodded mutely, still grasping onto my dreamy images of watching Rahul grow up, not believing either one of us at that point in time.

Sowmya's transition to Boston was hard for her. She moved with a five-month-old after giving up a very promising career in Delhi. We were concerned. Stepping off a promising career track is easy, but it can be hard to get back on. Khushi's decision to leave her college teaching job (a decision forced by me, I admit) came back to haunt her. But she kept her doubts to herself.

We waved goodbye through the glass walls of the Indira Gandhi Airport as Sowmya precariously made her way to the check-in counter, balancing Rahul in her left arm and pushing her luggage cart with her right, held back our emotions till she was out of sight, and crossed our fingers.

Paradoxically, even though Sowmya's move to Boston put her far away from us, over the next ten years we probably spent more time with her and got more deeply involved with the kids than we would have if she had stayed on in Delhi, as our lives took on an international, cross-cultural twist. Every year we made travel plans, followed by arrangements to close down our flat for the months we would be away – a request to MTNL to disconnect the phone line, deposits updated to maximize the interest income so critical to our finances, cheques signed in advance to pay electric bills, the postman told to re-route all our mail to Amiya's house, the carpet rolled up, the couches encased in sheets to minimize dust, the kitchen and the refrigerator emptied of all food, perishable or otherwise, the windows and screens closed, Gamaxin powder sprinkled strategically around the kitchen drains and periphery. Once we got over the tension of our preparations and firmly put aside concerns about all that could go wrong or would need to be fixed once we got back, we transitioned to a joyful few months spent in the U.S. with the kids.

Our first visit to Boston was in August 2000, when Atul was born, a year-and-a-half after Rahul. While Sowmya was in the hospital for a few days, we stayed with Rahul in the house. Khushi and I took the train with Rahul to Boston to see the new baby. It was quite an adventure. We had spent a lot of time telling Rahul he was going to have a new little brother. And now it was true, as we peered excitedly at chhota bhai in the nursery.

For the first time in my life, I spent whole days with small kids – reading the same alphabet books again and again, watching the same TV shows over and over, running the same little train on its wobbly plastic track all morning, and, best of all, taking an afternoon nap with Atul and Rahul both snuggled into the quilt with me. Even the fact that Rahul associated me with very basic activities, such as 'ga-bage' (I used to throw the garbage daily into the large trash container near the apartments) and 'cleanup' was fine with me. For the first time in my life, I was not offended at the thought of helping around the house. There was a joyful sense of release as my ego took a backseat, completely overwhelmed by the need to make these two very young people smile.

Rahul was 'Mr Okay'. He was a restless child, always thirsting for more – new books, new activities, new food. He was willing to try anything, always 'ok' with everything. Khushi and I were in Boston for Rahul's first day of preschool. Sowmya and Sharman were living in a sprawling apartment complex with an onsite preschool/daycare centre. Sowmya wasn't home on the day Rahul was to start, so it was up to Khushi and me to take him there. We packed his lunch and nervously dropped him off, relieved to see him happily run inside and start playing. When we went to pick him up a few hours later, he still looked happy, said bye to the teachers who were really pleased with his first day, but his lips were trembling. As soon as we walked out of the preschool area, he climbed into my lap and began to cry. He hadn't eaten all day. And since he was playing happily, no one had noticed. I was upset about that. Being somewhat old-fashioned, I didn't particularly like the idea of young kids being left in daycare or going to school too early. But this was a minor hiccup. Khushi showed Rahul how to open his lunch box and navigate all the items inside. We mentioned it at drop-off the next day. From then on, Rahul loved school, new books, new toys, new blocks, new friends, never looking back.

Atul was 'Mr No'. That was his first response to anything new. He preferred order, he didn't like change, he was most comfortable in his familiar environment. He did not like surprises sprung on him. He liked to be mentally prepared for anything new. If we were going somewhere, even if it was just to a restaurant for a meal, he would always say, 'Why didn't you tell me about this yesterday?' They were both happy children, but Atul was quieter, not as comfortable with strangers or new experiences.

The next year, it was decided that Atul would go to the daycare facility at the same preschool that Rahul went to and enjoyed, so that both brothers could be together. A month or so before we were supposed to return to India, Khushi and I took Atul there for the first time. Given the experience with Rahul, we were not prepared for what followed. Atul started to cry as soon as we got to the preschool and wouldn't let go of us. We sat with him for almost an hour before we somehow managed to transition him to the teacher's lap, where he continued to cry. And when we went back after a few hours, Atul was still crying. He had decided that he did not want to be there, and he was not going to try it. I felt very, very badly for him. It was traumatic dropping him off every morning. A few days later, we saw Atul pass by Sowmya's apartment with his preschool class. There was one teacher in front, one behind, and all the kids in the middle were trussed up in a harness. We spotted Atul, and he looked very sad as he walked past the apartment, glancing towards the French doors, hoping to see us. I felt like going outside, scooping him up and bringing him home, but I resisted.

After three weeks, nothing had changed. Sowmya and Sharman decided to withdraw Atul and have him stay with a neighbour, a kind lady with a teenage son who was looking for something to occupy her, and loved little kids. Being next door and with a familiar person was grudgingly acceptable to Atul. I heaved a sigh of relief, glad that things were settled before our planned return to India.

I loved my time with the kids. Rahul was a happy-go-lucky child, constantly absorbed in the wonders of the world, often chasing me around to read him whichever book he was fascinated with that day. Atul usually followed him around, mostly watching and copying him, always on the lookout for opportunities to trump his older brother. Khushi would take care of most of their needs, cooking for them, coaxing them to eat, teaching them some prayers while they rang the mandir bell. The task of entertaining them fell to me. I spent hours on the large white rug that dominated the living room with blocks, balls, trucks, and trains. As they got older, I taught them to play Ludo, Scrabble, chess. I learnt to balance my attention between them, casually step in when an unexpected altercation erupted, and treasure those precious days.

While they both came running to my arms, Atul showed a distinct preference for me, which was a little odd, very unexpected, and strangely flattering.

'No Nani,' he would say firmly, when Khushi handed him a sippy cup, looking at me intently till I took the sippy cup from Khushi and handed it to him. He would then smile contentedly, and accept it.

'Nana, nini,' he would insist when it was time for their afternoon nap, watching Khushi to make sure she did not take over.

'Nana, hand,' he would say, promptly grabbing my hand

when we headed out to the park, smiling victoriously at Rahul, who would be perfectly happy to hold Khushi's hand.

A year later, Atul started preschool, which was located in the same building where Rahul went to kindergarten. Atul was a little more accommodating now, and would go inside, but was still not completely happy with the idea of being left in a classroom. Khushi and I would walk the boys to school and back, since the school was a three-minute walk from the house. One day I wasn't feeling well, so Khushi went alone to pick up the boys.

'Where is Nana?' Atul asked immediately, stopping in his tracks, and glaring at Khushi when he saw her alone.

'He is at home. He wasn't feeling well,' she replied. 'Let's go.'

'No. I want Nana to pick me up. I will wait till he gets better,' said Atul, sitting down in the school hallway, refusing to move.

13

Seizure

'Wisdom is easy to learn but hard to practice.'

– Agastya Raj

August 2010

I feel my legs stiffen into a spasm. I wait for the uncomfortable stretch to go away, but it gains power, grasps me tighter, and creeps up my arms and torso. My head joins the action. I make no sound, waiting for someone to notice the imperceptible shifts under the covers. I ponder the deep irony of the ripple that runs through my body. *My body is abuzz with action ... action that is completely uncontrolled, and not noticeable to anyone. Instead of the joy of normal movement, it brings huge discomfort – first to me, and then, as soon as they notice, to everyone around me as they get thrown into despair.*

'Rahul,' yells Sowmya loudly. She has been sitting cross-legged on a chair next to me, savouring her stuffed paratha as usual, while I have been drifting in and out of my late morning nap, recovering from my morning schedule of tea, exercise, breakfast, shower – and mustering up energy to sip on the coconut water that will shortly arrive. Suddenly, my body stiffens further, and my neck jerks to one side.

'Rahul,' Sowmya yells again. 'Hold Nana's legs,' she continues as a confused young Rahul runs inside, followed by Atul. They each grasp one leg and try to keep them down as they jerk about, while Sowmya holds my arms and tries to keep my mouth open to make sure my tongue does not flop back and block my breathing. Khushi and Rajesh join them, everyone trying to calm me, or rather my body, down.

'Call the doctor,' says Sowmya. Before Khushi can find the phone number of the neighbourhood doctor in the small black phone diary, my body suddenly relaxes and I drift into a tired sleep.

* * *

October 2010

The summer heat is starting to subside. The ceiling fan is circling at medium speed. Sharman is here on a work trip for a few days and sitting next to me, telling me about the boys just starting a new grade in school. I am listening quietly when I feel the beginnings of a seizure. Everything begins to stiffen. I try to raise my hand, to tell him not to worry, that this has happened before, that it will go away. Everyone else who has seen this before jumps into action, holding me, waiting for the seizure to pass. After what seems like an eternity, I drift off in exhaustion, unaware that the seizure is still continuing.

I wake up shivering in a cool, dark room, a hushed silence interlaced with the mechanical beeping of instruments and the hissing of ventilators. It feels a little like Bed Number 6, but also different. My arms are freezing. I try my little mind game, wishing the blanket to move, but it remains stubbornly in place, tossed unevenly over my lower torso.

Khushi scurries in when the nurse informs her that I am awake, and starts rambling, bringing me up to speed

'The seizure did not go away, so we called the neighbourhood doctor. He suggested bringing you here to Ahuja Hospital. Do you remember the ambulance ride? They strapped you on a stretcher and brought you here. That's why you have those bruises on your arms. You have been sleeping for almost two days after they gave you a sedative.' I have obviously not seen the bruises till she lifts my arm and waves it gently in front of my eyes.

I spend a few days suspended in the chill of the ICU at Ahuja Hospital, not sure why I am here. Then I am transported back home with a cold, a feeling of complete exhaustion, a couple of small bed sores, a fuzzy growth behind my ears where the nurses consistently missed a spot through a week of sponge baths. I also have a new medical folder with a bunch of new prescriptions. An increased dose of the current anti-seizure medicine, as well as a new one which will probably keep me permanently wrapped in the mental fog that enveloped me during my week in the hospital. And a couple of antibiotics for the now raging urine infection and minor pneumonia I have acquired during my week's stay there. Khushi looks relieved to be back home.

'You look so much better' she says. *You and me both*, I agree.

'I think we should just stay here, let those doctors come to us instead,' she says half-jokingly, but watching intently for an imperceptible nod of agreement from me. She holds me tight as we make a joint decision, this time without a conversation. We slowly go back to our regular schedule, medications and therapy.

Seizures do happen, even a couple of times every week but like all situations which recur frequently, there is preparation, concern and immediate action, but no panic. When it happens, I look down at myself, my mind almost stepping outside my body, calmly waiting. Whoever is around makes sure my mouth stays open, usually with a spoon that is now always kept on the dressing table in a mug. When I wake up after the stuporous sleep that usually follows an exhausting seizure, I am relieved to not open my eyes to the cold air and low fluorescent lighting in a hospital ICU. I am still in my warm and friendly hospital-bedroom. We made a decision and are sticking with it.

14

The Mind Plays Tricks

*'Pretending you're ok is easier than explaining to
everyone why you're not.'*

– Unknown

1991–1997

The downward trajectory of my life began in April 1991.
I woke up feeling groggy, opening my eyes with great
difficulty. The noise level in and outside the apartment
told me that it was definitely later than my usual 5:30 a.m.
wake-up time. I looked at the clock. It said 9:30. *That can't
possibly be true – maybe it is 6:30*, I thought as I rubbed my
eyes. But I could hear the pressure cooker in the kitchen,
utensils clanking loudly. *How did I sleep through this racket?*

'You had an epileptic seizure last night,' said Khushi. She
had already booked an appointment with a neurologist
scheduled for 11 a.m., so I dressed quickly and ate my
breakfast, still a little surprised. Besides feeling a little tired,

I felt my usual healthy self. I had no recollection of having a seizure, a doctor being called, a Valium shot being given. After a series of tests, I was told that this was probably a random event and there was nothing to worry about. All was clear.

'There is a small injury at the base of the skull on one side. Sports injury, maybe?' mused the neurologist.

'I did climb a lot of trees in my village, I remember falling out of a few,' I replied jokingly. I went home with a six-month prescription for Dilantin, a standard anti-seizure medication. An uneventful six months and another battery of tests later, I stopped taking it. Life went on.

Unfortunately, that seizure was not the one-time event the doctors and everyone originally assumed. There were consequences that no one had anticipated. A few weeks after stopping the Dilantin, I was sitting in the drawing room drinking my tea when I had a strange sensation. The next thing I remembered was looking down at a large brown stain on my shirt, and a sensation of spreading warmth as tea was still trickling all the way down my leg to the floor.

Khushi was staring at me, puzzled. 'What happened? Did the mug slip? Was it too hot?' I shook my head, confused.

After a few days, it happened again. I was walking outside with my friend Mr Mehra when my mind briefly switched off.

'Raj?' Mr Mehra was saying repeatedly, while I could see Khushi scurrying over.

'Don't worry, Mr Mehra,' she said hurriedly. 'He just drifted off for a few minutes.' And added, by way of explanation – 'He should have had breakfast before his walk!'

And again. I was putting on the 8th green at the Army Golf Course when I sensed myself going blank. I shook my head, hoping for the best. The next thing I remember, I was standing on the 9th tee, Arvind urging me to tee off, since the other three had already taken their turn, and were looking at me, patiently waiting for me to emerge from my daze.

I went back to the neurologist, who was surprised, and diagnosed these events as 'complex absence seizures'. I went back on Dilantin, this time without the promise of being able to quit in six months. Dilantin prevents major seizures, but these mini-seizures were sneaky – they still burst through the calm shield created by the Dilantin around my brain. I continued the Dilantin anyway, maybe I had fewer mini-seizures than I would have otherwise, and maybe it prevented another massive episode. No one ever knows for sure, you only hope you are preventing something worse.

Every time it happened, it felt like I was groping in the dark frantically looking for the light switch, finding it, even pressing it continuously but being unable to switch it on. I was told that my expression changed, my words dissolved into a low guttural hum, I either stopped moving or repeated the same general movement over and over.

If you understand the problem, you can fix it, circumvent it, prevent it. I started pondering on the mini seizures. There seemed to be no trigger – activity, exhaustion, stress, location, weather. They seemed completely random, which was not a comforting thought. It would be so much better to know what caused these lapses into nothingness and turned my mind blank. But there was nothing. The strange thing was that I could almost sense them happening, but was helpless, almost like a mildly interested spectator who either could not or would not help. I began to tell myself I needed to keep it 'normal' when it happened, but was unsure about how I could do so.

In any case, we decided to go ahead and take a trip to the UK and US in 1993 that I had been saving up time and money for. This was Khushi's first foreign trip ever, and my first one since I came back to India in 1965. The trip was fun and thankfully uneventful. Soon after our return, it was obvious that the person substituting for me for the two months that I was away, had settled in as Regional Manager in the Delhi office, and was very keen to stay on. I was offered the option of taking on another region that was in trouble (I still had the reputation of being someone who could fix things and build something out of nothing) or another job at HQ in Madras. I was tempted to go back to Madras where I had started my India career, but a voice in my head stopped me.

Are you sure? said the voice. *What if … you blank out while you are talking in a meeting, or while you are signing a cheque, or while talking to customers?* I shuddered, playing it out in my mind. So far, I had been lucky. No one had noticed my short and imperceptible seizures, or maybe they had just not happened at an awkward time. The thought of it being noticed, whispered about, making its way around the company, being delicately and uncomfortably broached by Sam, my boss, was unnerving. I could not let that happen.

'I am thinking of retiring early,' I mentioned casually to Sam, my boss, when he came to Delhi for a meeting.

'Why, Raj – you must be joking. You can't retire before me!' said Sam, who had known me for thirty years and was more a friend than a boss.

'Well, I have been thinking. I am not sure I want to dive into something new in my career at this point, I want to relax, read, volunteer at the Chinmaya Mission, spend time with Khushi, maybe even improve my golf handicap which has not moved much in fifteen years!' I said, keeping my voice calm and thoughtful, actively rationalizing the decision in my head as I talked to him

'Why don't you come to HQ at Madras for a year? You can always retire if you don't enjoy yourself or still prefer to. Think about it,' he said, offering a reasonable option, still hoping to talk me out of what seemed like a rash decision.

Despite Sam's puzzled reaction and various attempts to

talk me out of or at least postpone the decision by a few months, I resigned, giving up not just my career but a company and colleagues who had been like family for thirty years. I could not show anyone how much the decision hurt me, how numb I felt while I tried to smile and continue to pretend that I was eager to retire and get working on my golf handicap. I told myself all the right things – this was the right decision, it was better to leave work with a respectful send-off rather that a potentially hurried departure if something embarrassing happened, I could now do everything I had been putting on the backburner all these years, I would anyway keep in touch with my colleagues, many of whom were friends, from work.

I got used to the fact that my memory lapsed, that it always happened without any warning and was completely random, and that it was just something I would 'have to live with'. And it went away, didn't it, without any material impact? But however much I ignored the episodes and carried on as if nothing had happened, each blank episode seemed to take away a little something of me – my thinking, my optimism, my confidence. And one episode took a larger bite.

I was driving to Tilak Nagar with some rajais that needed to be refilled with freshly spun cotton, getting them ready for winter. Khushi was chatting about our upcoming visit to Chintpurni when I suddenly felt a whooshing sound in my head, her voice became increasingly garbled and then, nothing.

I emerged to noise and chaos. My head was throbbing, nose resting awkwardly on the steering wheel. I raised my head, wincing in pain to see a cracked face staring at me through the windshield. I moved my head a bit, realizing the crack was actually in the windshield. I looked down to see Khushi's left foot sitting next to my right foot near the brake, her face right next to mine.

'I saw your face go blank,' she said quietly. 'I had to stop the car,' she continued by way of explanation. 'Are you OK?'

I nodded mutely, realizing that I had lost control of the car, and Khushi had quickly leaned over to push the brakes and stop the car. After that, I could no longer argue with Khushi when she pleaded with me to let her drive. She renewed her driving licence, started driving on short errands near the house, then started dropping and picking me up from the golf course three days a week. It was a minor scratch to the forehead, but a hard blow to my self-esteem.

My life slowed down dramatically after my early retirement. I slowly lost touch with my colleagues over the years, sometimes because of missed opportunities, but often due to my hesitation in reaching out and calling people, due to the niggling discomfort about people knowing. But beyond giving up my job, we were determined to not let our life come to a standstill. We went to Chintpurni a couple of weeks after the car accident, staying overnight and enjoying the morning darshan at our kuldevi, revisiting old times. I became keenly interested in Hindu philosophy, devouring all of Swami Chinmayananda's books with feverish interest, revisiting Vivekananda, reading Thoreau.

I started writing two diaries. One was my regular diary that just listed everything I had done during the day, my effort at memory maintenance and control. The other one was my spiritual diary, where I wrote my thoughts and interpretation of what I had read, what I had learnt and how I could apply it in my life. I guess you could say that I was now a religious person, except I was still not inspired to visit temples or attend jagrans. At most, I was more tolerant of them, and could go inside a temple with Khushi without feeling a strong urge to turn around and leave like I had done in Bhubhaneswar in the 1960s.

I became used to crossing my fingers behind my back every day, often many times a day. Khushi became used to watching me for signs, and saying a little prayer for my safety every time I stepped out of the house by myself, either for a walk in the park or to pick up milk at the kirana store. Neither of us once thought of constraining my activities and outings in order to play it safe. There was an unspoken fear in both our minds of what might happen if I had an episode while I was crossing the road, or if I slipped and fell, but we pushed it to the back of our minds. And every minute and hour and day and month and year since 1991, we have been thankful.

15

When You're in Bed, You're Dead*

*'Moment to moment, breath to breath, let your thoughts and
actions be in harmony with ground reality.'*

– Agastya Raj

November 2011

'We are going to the Golf Club!' My heart races at the
thought, an excited shiver coursing down my spine. It has
been one year and nine months since I stepped on the
green. And it is the first time ever Rajesh will be on a golf
course, he tells me excitedly after my bath as he lays out
my 'best' outfit for consideration. My sense of anticipation
is hard to suppress as he irons and polishes away.

*This must be the first time I will wear a formal white shirt,
formal grey trousers and black shoes on the golf course! I
shudder at the thought when Rajesh dresses me, wishing*

---

* The chapter title is inspired by the book *Tuesdays With Morrie* by Mitch
  Albom.

I could instruct him on more appropriate golf attire. But I let it go. He is excited for me, and looking forward to visiting one of those exclusive, elusive places he has never had a chance to see on the inside.

'We are going to be there in five minutes,' Sowmya, seated on my left, is talking to someone on the cell phone as we do a U-turn near Dhaula Kuan.

Wait a minute, we are driving past the main entrance, I think, my body leaning on Khushi on my right as the car does a sharp U-turn onto a dirt road instead of stopping at the main gate.

'You have special permission to enter through the gate that leads directly to the course,' says Sowmya. 'Most people have to walk through the main entrance and club-house area. Only deliveries and two-star generals get the honour of driving in!'

We drive down the dirt road along the brick retaining wall topped by a black railing fence along the boundary of the golf course, stopping briefly while the security guard squints at the number plate, compares it with his notebook and pushes open the giant metal gate. With the gate screeching shut behind us, we drive along an almost imperceptible service road, visible only as a lighter green ribbon of flattened grass meandering around the putting greens, and past the rabbit-cage near Hole 10. We stop near the club-house, next to the lower level coffee shop. One of the waiters is standing outside, and glances curiously at the car. I am so excited that I manage to completely shut out the embarrassment of being lift-dragged out of the car and onto the wheelchair, just keeping my eyes closed and willing it along while the transfer is happening.

Fast forward ten minutes, I am sitting comfortably in my wheelchair near the driving range, sipping a hot, sweet, frothy concoction from the small, plastic, disposable Nescafe cup and watching two people leisurely practicing their swing. *Good shot*, I say as I follow the ball that arcs through the sky and thuds down 200 metres away. I can feel my arms lifting themselves, gripping a golf club and swinging in sync with the older gentleman frowning as he focuses on his shot, our ears perked to hear the whoosh of that perfect swing, our eyes squinting in the direction of the ball's trajectory, hoping for a straight shot that clears the 150-metre sign, seeking that ever-elusive perfect shot.

For the next hour, I bask in the November sun, relishing the calming sights and sounds of my favourite place in the world. Khushi and Sowmya are sitting in plastic chairs next to me, Rajesh is walking around sipping his Nescafe. I soak up and bank away the visual and sensory experience, hoping my memory will hold it and allow me to replay it in my mind many times over. We wheel over to the coffee-shop, still sitting outside as I slowly savour the hot, steaming idli I am offered, reliving the laughter and conversation with my golf buddies over an omelette or idli–sambar that always followed our nine-hole game.

After two-and-a-half hours, I am still dreaming of the good old days, and barely notice the awkward struggle to heave me back into the car. I smile, or rather, flop my mouth, to show my happiness. *I can still feel really happy*, I think, wonderstruck by the thought. I hope I can come here again, and dare I hope I can swing a golf club again.

* * *

December 2011

The bee buzzing around my face has decided to rest on my nose. The desperate desire to flick away the annoying black speck I can see from the corner of my left eye is overwhelming. I can feel my legs stiffening as a response to my irritation as the bee flutters its silver wings. 'I'm in your face,' it seems to be saying. A spasm of pain shoots through my legs and beads of sweat form on my face as a burst of anger courses through me, quickly dissolving into the familiar sense of helplessness. *Is life really worth living, when one cannot swat a bee sitting on one's nose or even request someone to help in its removal?*

When we came home, there was a concerted and deliberate effort at normalcy, everyone pretended that I was participating fully in everything going on, everyone believed that this was a temporary phase we would all get through with a positive attitude. That sense of normalcy is still there, in fact it does not even seem forced, it is just the new normal. The only difference is that there is less talk about a future state where I will be walking and talking. And there is no mention of the fact that there has been no significant improvement in these many months.

Everything is about me, except I am not a part of it. Each day dissolves into the next. I am fed, shaved, bathed, exercised, read to, chatted with, played with, visited. The daily medicines, always on time. The antacid in the morning. The anti-seizure medicine after dinner. The homoeopathic pills that Khushi has complete faith in, always timed to be given fifteen minutes before a meal.

Khushi is tired, exhausted with the effort of keeping me going. While my life is in slow motion, in fact no motion, hers seems to have settled into a constant frenetic pace. Every day, I watch helplessly as her face ages rapidly, eyes receding deeper, cheekbones more visible, visible gulleys forming on both sides of her nose, new lines emerging as her skin thins and curls across her forehead. Her shoulders are a little stooped now, her neck hunching forward from constantly hovering over me. I see her toss and turn at night, wince and rub her knees when she wakes up, willing her body and mind to think and do everything that needs to happen every day.

* * *

February 2012

It has been an unusually warm February.

'Hello, Uncle,' says Sampreet, bustling in, her voice as bright and friendly as always, smiling and chatting while she gives me a professional look-over. She is Harveen's wife, and works as a general surgeon at a local hospital nearby. Since we came home in June 2010, she has been my visiting doctor, stopping by every few weeks on her way home from the hospital in the evening, and racing over for emergencies ever since we decided not to go to a hospital. She is the critical third corner of my care triangle.

Suddenly, there is a buzz of excitement outside my room. Amiya comes in, looking tired but animated. There is a fine layer of dust on what is usually a neat ponytail, making her hair a strange chalky yellow-brown colour. One corner of her dupatta is dirty and grimy, having clearly been used all day to wipe sweat off her face. She joins me for a cup of tea and recounts her visit to Rohtak to meet Babaji, an Ayurvedic practitioner who has 'cured' many stroke victims with his special treatment. To her, it was clearly worth the long trip in the car and even longer wait for an audience with Babaji. There is a fresh glimmer of hope on everyone's face.

'He does need to see you, though,' she says. 'He cannot prescribe any treatment without seeing you.'

Khushi is a little unsure. 'What do you think?' she says to me. 'We did decide not to go to a hospital, but this is different, all natural treatment, right? So there will be no side effects? And what do we have to lose?'

Suddenly plans are being made for the big trip – which days Babaji is available, when can we borrow the Santro from Devender, when can Rajesh come a half-an-hour early one day next week, etc., etc. By the time Amiya finishes her tea, it has been decided. We are going to Rohtak next week.

A few days later, I stare out of the window at the dust being kicked up by the two- wheelers, bicycles, and herds of goats that share the unfinished dirt road along the highway. My left shoulder is wedged against the door. My left arm has fallen from the position it was carefully placed in on my lap and is pulling my shoulder down with its dead weight, making it hurt. Amiya is sitting in the middle, propping me up on my right side. My body screams in pain and my legs go into a spasm. I focus on the hope.

The hustle and bustle, the heat and dust, the canvas-on-bamboo stretcher that is used to transport me from the car to Babaji's presence. Babaji is tall and stately, has long grey hair and a matching beard that flows into his white dhoti as he sits calmly among his people, under a shady tree. There is no attempt at privacy as my stretcher is placed gently on the floor in front of him. Babaji asks Khushi to describe what happened, and how I am doing.

She does, in great detail ending with her usual optimism – 'He is very stable, no infections, no major seizures, eating his meals, doing physical therapy.' *In other words, no crisis situations to grapple with, just a daily monotonous existence,* I think bitterly.

'I wish you had brought him earlier,' says Babaji, after instructing me to be rolled over and feeling his way down my spine and stroking my dead limbs. 'I have treated such cases with a special technique and medicine that stimulates the spinal nerves.'

Really? I think, my interest piqued. I study him with more interest. Wrinkled white dhoti and kurta, a thoughtful face, lined and leathered over seventy plus summers, sprinkled with salt-and-pepper stubble above the beard, glistening with sweat. He seems credible. He seems to care. He does not charge any money for consultation, just requests a donation for the medicines. *Why would he lie?*

Babaji dispatches his assistant to make the medicines as per his instructions. Meanwhile, he gives detailed instructions on how to apply the medicine. We leave with a big cloth bag full of goodies, after both Khushi and Amiya have bowed respectfully to Babaji and I have been transported back to the car via my makeshift stretcher.

The Ayurvedic treatment starts the next day, added to the time-table between my morning tea and shower. There is a heated mud pack mixed with the special medicines that has to be placed on my back for fifteen minutes. Then after my shower, there is a special oil that has to be massaged all over my body.

The biggest challenge is getting my back flat for the mud pack, an effort that requires multiple people to gently turn over my body on its stomach without injuring a floppy limb or squeezing the catheter. It hurts a lot, but I am willing to bear some discomfort for the promise of even some change in my existence.

There is a sense of excitement and renewed anticipation for the first few days, as we all pray for a miracle. I keep my eyes closed, and my face calm so that no one realizes how uncomfortable this is. *They might give up if they think I am hurting in any way.* I hush the skeptical little voice in my head that says – *Can a mud-pack really be the defibrillator that zaps your spinal nerves and brain back into action, after being in a suspended state for almost two years?*

By the end of the third week, I start giving up hope. The discomfort of the treatment, that I was willing to accept for the first few days, now seems annoying and unnecessary. Babaji had set a one-month window to assess positive impact from the special treatment, and we desperately look for any minor improvement we can report. 'If there was a change, come back for a refill of the medication,' Babaji had said.

What he meant was, *if there is no improvement in a month, it is probably too late.*

Clearly, we are not going to go back.

Author's Note

Writing this book has been a therapeutic experience, helping me deal with a roller-coaster of emotions – confusion, denial, hope, frustration, grief, regret, but also pride and joy. As I have stepped into what I imagine is a seething cauldron of emotions as he struggles with a personal calamity, I have tried to capture and represent my father's personality – thoughtful, positive, calm, and never depressing.

This is a story about relationships – spousal commitment, family support, the parent–child bond. This is a story about respect – for everyone, whatever state they might be in, however limited their physical or mental ability. This is a story about resilience – working with what life throws at you, with a smile on your face. This is a story about realism – dealing with tough situations positively, understanding that effort does not always yield the results one hopes for, but still continuing the effort.

I hope it made you pause, to acknowledge, and appreciate the key relationships in your life. I hope it made you think about your parents as people, beyond critiquing them as the people who brought you up. I also hope it made you think about how you view and interact with people who are not fully functional, and deliberate on the grey area between living and existing, which is defined by attitude, not physical and mental status.

I hope this book will resonate with people who have dealt with difficult life situations, and sensitize those that have not, making them better prepared for life's curveballs.

Cast of Characters

Primary character: Agastya Raj – named after Sage Agastya, pet name Bhiga, common name Raj, youngest of one sister and three brothers

Other characters:

Alok – Raj's friend in UK, and later colleague in Madras

Amanda – Raj's first crush

Amar – colleague in UK, and later in Madras

Amiya – Khushi's youngest sister

Arvind – Raj's golf buddy, one of the regular foursome

Atul – Raj's younger grandson

Babaji – a practitioner of natural medicine

Baldev – Raj's older brother

Ben – Raj's college friend

Bhabho – Raj's mother

Biji – Khushi's mother

Biraji – Raj's father

Braj – Vyom's older brother

Chachaji – Raj's grand-uncle, controlled the family business

Chhote Chachaji – Raj's uncle

Deepti – Nitin's daughter

Devender – Amiya's husband

Dharmender – Raj's childhood friend

Harveen – son-like doctor, respected Raj as a father figure, also Sampreet's husband

Jeet – colleague in UK, and later in Madras

Jhaiji – Uma's mother

Khushi – Agastya's wife, oldest of six sisters and three brothers

Manoj – colleague in UK, and later in Madras

Master Umruddin – teacher at village school

Mata Ram – blind man in the village, who relied on community support for survival

Mr Joshi (the physiotherapist) – he worked with Raj daily for two years

Mr Joshi (the speech therapist) – he worked with Raj after his first stroke

Nawaz – driver who had been with the family for many years

Nitin – Khushi's youngest brother

Pitaji – Khushi's father

Rahul – Raj's older grandson

Rajesh – home attendant who took care of Raj for two years

Sam – Raj's colleague, boss and friend

Sampreet – daughter-like doctor who took care of Raj's medical needs for two years, also Harveen's wife

Sharman – Sowmya's husband

Sohan – Uma's brother

Sowmya – Khushi and Raj's daughter

Sukhdev – Raj's oldest brother

Sushma Chachi – Raj's aunt, Chhote Chachaji's wife

Uma – Baldev's (Raj's brother) wife

Varun – Baldev and Uma's son

Vyom – Raj's childhood friend

Glossary of Indian Terms

Aarti – a Hindu song/hymn dedicated to a deity, often performed with lighted lamps, flowers, fruits and other offerings

Agarbatti – incense sticks

Akhaara – old-fashioned wrestling gym, popular in Punjab

Amaanat – treasure, something held in trust

Angithi – coal-based traditional brazier used for space heating or cooking

Baithak – sitting room, living room

Balika Vadhu – a TV series that traces the arduous journey of a child bride

Bara chokra – 'big boy'; used to refer to an older helper/servant

Baraat – a celebratory wedding procession that escorts the groom, who is traditionally on horseback, to the bride's home

Bare Papa – 'older father'; used to refer to an older uncle as a sign of respect

Berra – courtyard

Besan barfi – dessert made of gram flour, sugar, and ghee (clarified butter)

Beta – son; lovingly used to refer to a child of any gender in Punjab

Bhagavad Gita – a sacred Hindu text composed about 200 BC that contains the teachings of Lord Krishna to Arjun on the battlefield of Kurukshetra in the Mahabharata

Bhajan – devotional song or hymn

Bidaai – farewell, send off for a bride to her in-laws house after the wedding

Chai – tea

Chappal – slippers

Char dham – 'four pilgrimage sites' that Hindus believe helps achieve salvation; Badrinath (north), Dwarka (west), Rameswaram (south), and Puri (east)

Chhat – terrace

Chhole bhature – chickpea curry and fried Indian bread; popular Indian fast food

Chhota bhai – little brother

Chhota chokra – 'small boy'; used to refer to a younger helper/ servant

Chuha – mouse

Dada – grandfather (father's father)

Dadi – grandmother (father's mother)

Dahi – curd, yogurt

Dal – lentil curry

Dalia – cracked wheat cereal, often cooked with milk and sugar

Darshan – viewing god, especially in a temple

DDA – Delhi Development Authority; government body in charge of land development in India's capital city that designed and built many neighbourhoods and flats

Dhokla – seasoned and steamed chickpea flour snack

Dhoti – loose, unstitched piece of clothing worn on lower half of the body by men

Didi – older sister; often used to address anyone slightly older in a respectful way

Divan – a backless sofa or couch, designed to be set against a wall

Diwali – Hindu festival of lights; also associated with the Ram's arrival to Ayodhya after rescuing Sita from Ravan. Also honours Lakshmi, the goddess of wealth

Doaba – land between two rivers; refers here to the Bist Doab, the land between the Sutlej and Beas rivers

Dupatta – long, light scarf worn around the neck, shoulder or head

Durbar – grand hall or place of audience; an official reception or audience held by a ruler

Dussehra – Hindu festival marking the triumph of Ram over the 10-headed demon king Ravan, who abducted Ram's wife, Sita. Dussehra also signals the culmination of the nine-day Navratri festival

Dwar – gate, entrance

Gali – alleyway, small street

Ganga jal – sacred water from the river Ganga (Ganges)

Gobhi paratha – flat unleavened bread that is stuffed with cauliflower (gobhi) and fried on a griddle

Guli danda – popular street game played with a small ball (guli) and stick (danda)

Gutli – the centre core of a mango

Halwa – popular confectionery, here refer to a soft version made with roasted semolina cooked in butter and sugar syrup

Hatti – shop, location of family business

Havan – Hindu ritual where special offerings are made to a holy fire to invoke blessings for a special occasion

Hukka – single- or multi-stemmed instrument for heating or vaporizing, then smoking

Idli-sambhar – steamed rice cake (idli) with spicy lentil curry (sambhar)

Imarti – dessert made by deep-frying skinned black gram flour batter in a circular flower shape and soaking it in sugar syrup

Jagran – 'staying awake'; refers to an all-night prayer session with hymns and songs

Janam patri – horoscope

Janamashtami – Lord Krishna's birthday

Jija(ji) – brother-in-law, specifically sister's husband; (ji) is a suffix commonly added to names, titles to address someone respectfully

Jitey raho – 'may you live long'; a blessing

Kabaddi – a game played between two teams of seven players, in which individuals take turns to chase and try to touch members of the opposing team without being captured by them

Kangna – bracelet; refers here to a special knotted bracelet a bride is wearing when she comes to her in-law's home, where the knots are released for good luck

Khaat – Also known as charpoy, a traditional bed, consisting of a wooden frame strung with canvas or light rope

Khaata – record book; register used for keeping accounts

Khichdi – a gruel like dish comprising rice and lentils, and often vegetables

Kirana – local grocery store

Kuldevi – clan goddess

Kurta – loose shirt-like garment like a shirt without a collar worn in the Indian sub-continent

Laddoo – round Indian dessert, usually made of chickpea flour globules and sugar, popular for auspicious occasions

Maidan – a large park; an open space used for meetings and sports

Mandap – temporarily erected frame structure; usually decorated with flowers, used for wedding ceremonies

Mandir – temple, prayer area

Martvan – earthen pot with a lid

Masala chai – tea brewed with ginger, cardamom and other spices

Matha teko – 'forehead down', pay obeisance at the altar of god, usually by touching head to the ground as a sign of respect

Mela – fair or festival

Mera dar khula hai, khula hi rahega, tumhare liye – 'my door is open, it will remain open, for you'; lyrics from a song in the film *Purab aur Paschim (East and West)*

Mother Dairy – chain of outlets selling milk, other dairy products and vegetables in Delhi

MTNL – Mahanagar Telephone Nigam Ltd, a government-run telephone company in Delhi and Mumbai

Muhurat –the auspicious moment to start something new

Mukut – crown, headgear

Murga – 'chicken'; punishment where a child has to squat and hold their ears

Namaste – greeting

Nana – grandfather (mother's father)

Nani – grandmother (mother's mother)

Nastik – atheist, non-believer

Navratri – 'nine nights'; major festival held in honour of the divine feminine. Ends with Dussehra

Nini – sleep, nap

Om Ganeshaya Namah – In praise of Lord Ganesha

Pakora – fritters made with assorted vegetables, and chickpea flour batter

Panchayat – 'council of five'; a village council traditionally comprised of village elders

Pande Nivas – the Pande homestead

Papad – a thin wafer made of dried lentil, that is fried or roasted and eaten with meals

Parantha – a flat unleavened bread that is fried on a griddle

Pathis – dried cowdung cakes often lining the walls of rustic houses as a cheap thermal insulator and insect repellant, and used as a replacement for firewood in cooking stoves

Phera – circumambulation of the holy fire to consecrate a Hindu wedding

Pinni – a round dry sweet made from ghee, wheat flour, jaggery, and nuts, very popular in winter; very nutritious

Prasad – a devotional offering made to a god, typically consisting of food, fruits, sweets or nuts, that is later shared among everyone present

Puja – prayer

Rajai – quilt, filled with spun cotton

Rajender Kumar – popular and successful Bollywood film actor in the 1960s

Rajma chawal – kidney bean (rajma) curry and rice (chawal)

Ramayan – Ramayan is one of the two major Sanskrit epics of ancient India, that narrates the life of Rama, prince of the legendary kingdom of Kosala

Rath yatra – chariot race

Ravan – the demon king of Lanka in the ancient Sanskrit epic Ramayana, widely considered to be a symbol of evil due to his kidnapping of Sita, but also considered a great ruler and learned scholar

Roti – unleavened bread cooked on a griddle

Saag – spinach and other leafy vegetables

Sabzi – vegetables

Sahib – 'Sir'; often used as a sign of respect

Samosa – Deep fried pastry with a savoury filling, such as spiced potatoes, meats, or lentils, typically shaped like a triangle

Sari – women's garment from the Indian subcontinent that consists of an unstitched drape that is typically wrapped around the waist, with one end draped over the shoulder

Sarson – mustard, often refers to cooked mustard greens

Serai – guest house

Shami kebab – a typical South Asian kebab, flat in shape and fried, rather than grilled

Shavasan – Corpse pose, a yogic posture of blissful neutrality that is intended to rejuvenate the body, mind, and spirit, and release

Sita – wife of Lord Ram in the epic Ramayan, who gets kidnapped by Ravan

Sukh Sagar – Hindi translation of the Bhagavad Gita

Takht – sofa, long bed, bench

Tava – iron griddle used to make unleavened bread

Thali – large metal plate with curved edges used for meals

Tulsi – holy basil, has antiseptic properties

Upanishads – Sanskrit sacred texts probably composed between 400 BC and 200 BC, embodying the mystical and esoteric doctrines of ancient Hindu philosophy

Vividh Bharati – Indian government-run radio channel run by All India Radio. It has 40 stations across India, running since 1957, and telecasts a lot of entertainment programmes, especially music

About the Author

Rima Pande lives in the Boston area, enjoys parenting three amazing kids, unstructured and experimental cooking, and maximum travel. Her favourite leisure activity is sitting outside in an Adirondack chair with a book when it is sunny and 22 degree celsius.